LAST SEEN

Wesley Hisao Higaki

PROLOGUE

Sunday, March 7

As soon as she stepped through the gateway, the blonde felt eyes on her. An icy tingle crept through her body like a slow static electric current; the hairs on the back of her neck rose; her skin prickled. Her eyes moved up to the surveillance cameras mounted along the walls. The silent, omnipresent, electronic sentries of Homeland Security recorded her every step, every movement through the concourse. Or was someone else watching?

Meghan took a deep breath. The air in Northern California smelled fresher than in Los Angeles — the welcome scent of home. She pushed past the other passengers at Gate 20, turned right, towing her red roll-aboard luggage as she glided along the Terminal B concourse in San Jose's Norman Y. Mineta International Airport.

She had returned on the last flight into SJC after a weekend trip in Los Angeles to attend her grandmother's 80th birthday party. The last of the night's departing flight announcements came through the overhead public address system, echoing off the walls. The midnight curfew benefited residents living near the noisy metropolitan airport.

In celebration of the grande dame, those near and dear to Grandma gathered at a lavish affair. With all her aunts and uncles in attendance, Meghan chatted with her father's relatives whom she hadn't seen in years.

Aunt Marybeth, her father's youngest sister, came to the party drunk and danced on a table, an amazing feat considering the woman, in her fifties, weighed over 200 pounds. Aunt Patricia, a card-carrying cougar, flirted with every single guy at the party. Uncle Greg, Dad's older brother, and his wife, Charlene, church choir members, led the gathering in singing an off-key rendition of "Happy Birthday" to Grandma. Those spectacles were common at Harper family gatherings and the reason Meghan's parents excused themselves from the festivities.

Her parents gave their usual excuses for not flying out from Denver. Dad was too busy with work, even though it was his mother's birthday. Last-minute preparations for a benefit concert to raise money for a Denver-area homeless shelter demanded Mom's attention. She never missed the social events she had planned.

It was better they didn't attend. Meghan didn't need the added drama their presence would have caused. Their constant demeaning comments about their relatives' behavior grated on her. Grandma didn't ask about them. If her son's antics annoyed Grandma, she never let on. She seemed to accept the way they were. Meghan wasn't so forgiving.

The Stanford University junior had made personal sacrifices to attend. Maintaining a 4.0 GPA demanded much of her available time, but reserved weekends for having fun — and making money. That weekend, she played the role of the good granddaughter even if she wasn't, according to her mother, always the perfect daughter.

She studied chemistry and wanted to attend med school after Stanford, although she hadn't decided what field of medicine, perhaps pediatrics; she liked kids. She was determined to get into a competitive school and pay for it herself — free of her parents' financial umbilical cord.

Meghan bought Grandma a silk scarf in emerald - her favorite color - from a San Francisco designer. Meghan was delighted the scarf complimented the outfit Grandma wore that day. She received kudos from her relatives for her excellent taste and sense of style — a skill she'd honed through her side business.

Thanks to 9/11, every airport she'd been in since she could remember had cameras, security screening checkpoints, X-ray machines, and TSA agents. All the Federal government surveillance couldn't rival her mother's watchful eye. Ever since she was a child, her mother controlled her every move. Did her mother have access to airport video feeds? She waved to the camera, just in case.

Thoughts of security reminded her of a promise she'd made to her best friend. Meghan stopped before exiting the concourse and leaned against a pillar next to the departures board to text her roommate, Alexis, letting her know she had landed safely and was heading home. Over-protective Alexis. Meghan was a big girl and could take care of herself. The airport was a secure place with omnipresent cameras and guards; no need for Alexis to worry. But a promise was a promise, and it took Meghan only two seconds to tap out the electronic message. She pocketed her phone, grabbed her luggage handle, and rode the escalator down to the baggage claim and arrivals area.

When she reached the ground floor, her phone pinged, a new message on her private messaging app. As she read the message, her heart leapt.

r u here?

She thumbed an eager response. *Just landed.*

A moment later, a proposal. *I promised you some adventure. Game?*

Meghan had dated this man several times and enjoyed their encounters. He lavished fine meals and gifts on her. She had fun. His promise of adventure titillated her. She ached for some special excitement with him. Her thumbs flew. *Yes, absolutely.*

He replied with a time and place to meet. She sent her acknowledgement. It was a date.

Meghan ducked into the nearest restroom to change out of her jeans, sweatshirt, and running shoes. It took a few minutes to apply fresh makeup, fix her hair, and put on a new outfit. When she emerged, men's hungry eyes ogled her, pupils dilated, twisting their heads like owls as she walked past. Her form-fitting Ford dress, four-inch Louboutin stilettos, and a 24-karat gold bracelet elicited the reaction she wanted. Heat rose to her cheeks. She craved the attention — it provided validation.

Meghan needed a ride to her rendezvous point. She had left her car at home — traffic congestion and airport parking hassles had kept her from driving to the airport. Cabs were unreliable. Like millions of riders, she preferred rideshares. Quick, convenient, easy. The rare news reports about attacks on female riders didn't faze her.

Meghan whipped out her phone again, opening her rideshare app. A car was available three minutes away. Good. She didn't want to stand out in the late-night chill in her thin dress any longer than necessary. She confirmed the ride and strode to the exit.

Her heels clacked as she slipped past the automatic doors onto the sidewalk outside the terminal. A gentle breeze ruffled the hem of her skirt, tickling her thighs. She scampered across the street to the island designated for public transit and rideshare pickups.

Her ride pulled up to the curb in front of her, a silver Honda Accord. It looked like it had been recently washed and waxed. Meghan bent at the waist and peered inside. A rumpled newspaper and an open paperback lay on the front passenger seat, a Coke can with a straw in the cup holder.

The driver leaned toward the open passenger window. "Meghan?"

Alexis might have been over-cautious in having her text her when she landed, but Meghan followed reasonable rules of caution, especially when dealing with strangers. Meghan examined the driver's dashboard identification card, comparing it to the information on her app. Everything checked out.

"Yes." She opened the rear door, shoved her luggage in first, and climbed into the car. She caught her driver staring in his mirror; his wide, unblinking eyes looked like golf balls in the middle of his brown face. He looked away when she glared back at him.

The driver double-checked the destination on his app and asked, "Are you sure about this address? It's pretty far away." He twisted in his seat; his gaze fixed on her cleavage.

He leered at her like a ravenous tiger salivating over a piece of raw meat. Meghan's skin crawled; alarms clanged in her head. Other men had given her that same look — it spelled trouble. As she reached for the door handle to escape, her phone pinged with another message from her impatient date.

r u coming?

Her heart raced; anxious anticipation replaced her trepidation. She thumbed a hasty reply. *On my way.*

She fastened her seatbelt. "That's right," she said to the driver. "Can we hurry? I don't want to keep him waiting."

The driver smirked and nodded. He faced forward, put the car in gear, and drove away from the curb, joining the flow of outbound traffic headed toward the freeway.

Meghan gazed through her window into the darkness. The night promised to be memorable.

ONE

Sunday, March 21

Jake drove his subcompact rental car south along Highway 101 toward San Jose after arriving on a flight from Washington, D.C. an hour earlier. He'd flown into San Francisco International Airport dozens of times to meet clients in the tech-rich Santa Clara County region known as Silicon Valley. No need for GPS; the familiar route was a straight shot from SFO to San Jose, the largest city in the San Francisco Bay Area, host to the 12th Annual International Cybersecurity Conference. Jake planned to attend CyberSec technical sessions and visit vendor exhibition booths during the week-long trade show, but his primary goal was to meet clients and win some consulting contracts.

Jake parked his car in front of his hotel and climbed out. The convention center stood across the street with a ten-by-twenty-foot LED marquee flooding the area with light announcing the CyberSec Conference. He popped the trunk and extracted his suitcase. Jake sighed as he thought about the miles he would cover trudging the concrete floors of the convention center hunting for leads during the week.

"Jake! How are you?" Prof. Jean Stafford smiled as she emerged from the hotel with a group of men. She gave Jake a hug.

"Professor! I'm doing well. You look terrific!" Jake stepped back from the short-haired brunette. It had been a decade since she was his grad school advisor and three years since he'd seen her at another trade show.

"Are you still at John Adams?"

"I'm on leave right now. I'm focusing on my consulting business."

Consulting with companies and government agencies on how to improve their cybersecurity defenses became his full-time job since he'd taken a break from his adjunct teaching job at John Adams University in Georgetown. Lately, he'd spent less time preparing lessons and grading papers, and more time wooing clients.

"I see. I bet the mall incident helped give you some advertising."

Jake had quit teaching after gaining notoriety for thwarting a terrorist attack. Clients came out of the woodwork clamoring for his services. His proverbial fifteen minutes of fame stretched to six months. Jake took advantage of his newfound celebrity to expand his business. Unfortunately, he took on too much debt, too quickly. When the fickle news media moved on to new heroes and the public got distracted by other issues, his popularity waned, leaving him with fewer clients and massive bills.

Jake nodded. "Government budget cuts in cybersecurity have limited the opportunities. That's why I'm here at the conference wooing commercial clients."

CyberSec Conference was the ideal place to fish for potential customers. Conference organizers expected 50,000 attendees — all searching for solutions to their knotty cybersecurity problems. Some had arrived ahead of Jake, attending sponsored social functions at the local bars and restaurants before the official conference activities began.

"Jean! You coming?" a man from her group yelled.

"Yes!" She hollered back like a construction worker. She turned to Jake and said, "Good luck this week. I'm glad I ran into you." She scampered to rejoin her cohorts.

Jake watched the group blend into the crowd on the busy sidewalk. Conference attendees, residents, and tourists strolled outside the hotel. Besides the conference, downtown San Jose venues hosted a rock concert at the arena across the Guadalupe Freeway and a musical at the performing arts center a few blocks away. The shows released pedestrians and motorists into the neighboring streets. Jake didn't have time to partake in any of those amenities; he had work to do.

He closed the trunk, handed his keys to the valet, and entered the hotel. How much were they charging for parking?

The next morning, Jake woke at 5:00 AM — his body was still on Eastern Time. Daylight Saving Time had just kicked in, and the skies were pitch-black; sunrise not due for two hours. He went downstairs to the hotel's fitness center. Half-a-dozen guests, an equal number of men as women, sweated and chuffed through their workouts. Jake hopped onto an open treadmill and jogged at an 8-minute-per-mile pace. Lately, he had been lax in his fitness regimen and vowed to reclaim it despite his work and travel schedule. The exercise helped clear his mind, but a nagging thought entered at mile two.

Before he left on his trip, Jake and his daughter, Kenzie, a high school junior, had discussed which colleges she wanted to attend. Raised on the east coast, Ivy League schools were at the top of her list. She also liked Stanford. All expensive institutions. Jake's ex-wife, Samantha, reminded him he needed to contribute more to Kenzie's college fund. He couldn't disagree. He didn't spoil his daughter, but he wanted Kenzie to have the best education, which meant generating more income. Closing some lucrative deals at the conference would be a critical step toward that goal.

At 6:00, he returned to his room to shower, shave, and dress for a 7:00 AM breakfast meeting with a potential client, representatives from an Internet start-up interested in hiring him to improve the security of their systems.

On his way through the hotel restaurant to his meeting, Jake overheard snippets of diners' conversations. Three guys in suits sat at a table tossing jargon between them: market share, profitability, time-to-market. He slowed as he passed a booth of men in t-shirts and jeans.

"Our systems use AES-128 encryption for all the data transmissions," boasted the shaggy-haired guy.

"Yes, but does it have the U.S. Government FIPS-140 certification? If it hasn't been certified, how can I believe your claims?" countered the guy to his left.

Jake smirked. They spoke his language, obviously CyberSec attendees.

He reached his table and sat with the two men and a woman from Excelatron, a two-year-old, Sunnyvale-based company funded by well-respected venture capital firms. Excelatron delivered cloud services to small-to-medium-sized businesses. A long-term engagement with them would be a fruitful start for Jake's west coast trip. Their booth in the back of the restaurant offered the illusion of privacy. They felt comfortable talking about the sensitive topic.

"I've heard a lot about you in the news, Mr. Granger," said Petra Michaels, Excelatron's CEO.

"Pleased to meet you, Petra." Jake shook her hand, cool and soft; but her grip was firm. "Call me Jake. I'm guessing that's how you learned about me."

Jake joined the U.S. Army immediately after high school. After bootcamp, he joined Army Intelligence and gained real-world experience with cybersecurity. He learned to use the tools of the trade to assess systems, detect and defend attacks, and identify and locate attackers. He left the Army and attended Carnegie Mellon University to learn the theory behind the work he did in the military and received a master's degree in computer science. While in school, he parlayed his schoolwork and practical experiences into a consulting business, catering to the same government organizations and people he dealt with while in the Army. Word-of-mouth drove most of his business, but fortune offered him some welcome publicity.

"Jake, you stopped that terrorist attack at the Crossroads Mall. That was quite a feat." Petra smiled. "You must be some kind of natural-born hero. I read you saved three hundred lives that day," she gushed, looking at Jake like a teenager gazing at a Justin Timberlake poster on her pink bedroom wall.

"I'm no hero. I was just trying to save my daughter; anyone would do that, protect their family."

The media published the story about Jake's heroic exploits, stopping the madman from destroying the popular shopping mall with a bomb in his daughter's backpack. There was no avoiding the notoriety, dozens of eyewitnesses with mobile cameras streaming the action live online and dozens of security cameras capturing each step taken by the terrorists and Jake. The official count of people saved was one hundred thirty-two, including Jake and Kenzie. Homeland Security classified and buried the story about how Jake saved the life of a U.S. congressman earlier that day.

"Let's get down to business. Our investors are concerned," interrupted Amar, the VP of product development. "They want us to have a greater focus on cybersecurity. We handle a lot of sensitive customer information and we want to take the appropriate precautions."

"To tell the truth, hackers attacked one of our competitors and accessed an undisclosed amount of customer data. They've spent a shitload of effort and money trying to recover from the media firestorm that followed. Customers got nervous and some of their investors pulled out," Kevin, the VP of marketing, added.

"That sounds like fortuitous news for you," Jake commented as he stuffed a forkful of scrambled eggs into his mouth. He followed it with a gulp of bitter black coffee.

"On the surface, you'd think so, but we don't want to make the same mistake they did," Amar replied.

"Our investors agreed and said we need to do more to bolster our cyber defenses before our customers start worrying and before we get hacked. We don't know what to do — it's not our core expertise," said Petra.

Jake rubbed his hands together. This opportunity sounded like a long-term engagement with lots of consulting hours. He licked his lips as he thought about the money rolling into his coffers. Princeton, Cornell, Harvard, or Stanford could be part of Kenzie's future.

"What I'd suggest is an initial assessment. I'd do an asset analysis and threat profile. Then a risk analysis..." Jake began.

"Well," interrupted Amar. "We thought about something more like a pen test." Amar glanced at Petra, who nodded her approval.

Jake frowned. "A penetration test?"

"You know. You try to hack our systems," mansplained Amar. "Where I used to work, we hired an ethical hacker to penetrate our defenses and tell us where the weaknesses were. It worked out great for us."

Jake raised his eyebrows at Amar's use of the term "ethical hacker", an oxymoron of sorts. Organizations hired people to attack their systems and networks to identify vulnerabilities. Jake performed this task hundreds of times for clients, but he never liked the term, "ethical hacker". Jake preferred "white hat" to differentiate from those who were "black hats" or malicious hackers. He was sure Amar had picked up the term somewhere and didn't really understand what it entailed.

The conversation reminded Jake of teaching his freshman-level computer science classes. These executives were naïve, exemplifying the adage: a little knowledge was a dangerous thing.

"Penetration testing is an important activity to ensure security, but it's only a minor part of a much broader strategy that I'm more than happy to help you develop. Like I said, I think it would be prudent to start with an assessment…"

"Sorry. Our investors want to see results now. We think if we show them the results of a pen test, we can prove we are in good shape," interrupted Petra. Her subordinates nodded.

"Perhaps if I spoke with your chief security officer…" Jake began.

"We don't have a CSO — yet. I'm acting in that capacity," remarked Amar, grinning as if his brilliant smile might obscure his ignorance.

"To be honest, our budget for this is about $10K. Do you think you can do a thorough pen test with that?" Kevin asked. His honesty and naivete grated on Jake.

The miniscule offer deflated Jake. Thoughts of sending Kenzie to an Ivy League school vanished. Ten thousand dollars would barely pay his travel expenses from the east coast. Jake looked down at the remnants of his breakfast: cold eggs, half-eaten toast, and a slice of cantaloupe. He chewed his lower lip.

"We could sweeten the pot with some stock grants vesting over two years," said Petra. She leaned in and whispered, "Between you and me, we expect to go IPO in a year."

Jake's built-in lie detector kicked in; an inherent skill he honed through years of practice in the Army and in his consulting work. The experts called it reading body language and micro-expressions. Jake called it listening to his gut. Facial tics, posture, blinking, speech patterns. He couldn't explain how he could tell. He sensed the lies.

Petra blinked faster than when she talked about their situation with hackers. Her eyebrow twitched. Even her partners looked uncomfortable, glancing away, fidgeting. She looked expectantly at Jake.

Petra's offer was an empty promise. Jake didn't need his internal lie detector to figure out their stock grants were worthless. There was a one-in-ten-thousand chance their company would go public; a slimmer chance they'd be acquired. The probability their stock grants would be worth anything was slim. Their financials were secret, but they had announced their first-round funding of $20M two years ago. A solid sum, but nothing since. Jake sensed a cash flow problem. Their security project was probably one of many they needed to complete to win another round of funding.

Stock grants in a Silicon Valley start-up led by the likes of the people sitting in front of him gave Jake no confidence this endeavor would be profitable.

Jake sat in the conference's main assembly hall with three hundred attendees for the opening keynote speeches. It was like waiting for the start of a rock concert: loud music, strobing lights. Jake's meeting with the Excelatron execs was a bust. He politely told them he'd consider their offer, but it was a money-losing proposition. He had other client meetings that week. He hoped those would be more fruitful.

The conference's keynote speaker slot was traditionally a CEO of a platinum-level sponsor promoting his company's approach to cybersecurity, but this year's opening speaker was Nigel Brookside, the so-called "Father of Internet Security" and Jake's former commander in the Army. The CyberSec organizers were fortunate to land the industry's elder statesman. Nigel often passed up speaking at commercial tradeshows, favoring academic events. "More intellectual," he'd told Jake.

After the stirring keynote speech, Jake strode along the convention center corridor toward the conference room for his first technical session, a panel discussion entitled, "The Security Implications of the Ubiquity of the Internet." The panel featured an Air Force colonel, a director from the NSA, a distinguished engineer from Microsoft, and a VP from Cisco. Jake expected each to present a unique perspective on the topic and provide plentiful fodder for a lively debate. In the past, too many sessions devolved into veiled marketing pitches for the speaker's company's products.

The panel discussion room was at the end of the long, wide corridor, lined with posters announcing the session tracks; television monitors flashed sponsors' ads and news updates. The crowd, a mix of suits, jeans, and a few uniforms, young and middle-aged, mostly male, pressed through the hallway. The throng grew denser as he approached his destination. He picked up his pace to get to the meeting room early to claim a seat at the front of the room.

"Jake! Jake Granger!" a voice from behind boomed.

Jake twisted his head and saw a man in his twenties waving to him through the crowd. Jake scrunched his face. Did he know this man? From where? A potential customer? Jake stopped — the panel session could wait if it meant making a connection to a new client.

"Jake Granger," the man gasped. "I'm glad I caught up with you."

Jake studied the stranger, straining to recall his acquaintance. Five-foot-nine. Long, sandy blond hair, blue eyes. Tan camel hair jacket and matching slacks. Nothing registered. Who was he?

The man stuck out his hand. "I'm Tim McGuire. I'm a tech reporter from the Stockton Daily News."

Jake shook Tim's hand. Stockton? The city in California's Central Valley? "Do I know you?"

"No, but I know you. I've been following your story since the Crossroads Mall incident."

"Really?" Jake glanced over his shoulder and watched attendees file through the door to his session. So much for finding a front-row seat. "What can I do for you…. Tim?"

Tim handed him his business card. "I'd like to interview you. I'm interested in your business, your clients, your projects. The world of cybersecurity is fascinating, and I think our readers would enjoy your insights."

Stockton was 75 miles to the east of Silicon Valley in an area known for farming, not computers. Jake didn't understand why those readers would be interested in computer hackers when he imagined their newspaper contained articles about the drought, crop production, and fertilizer prices. He didn't have time to argue.

"I have to run. I don't want to miss my session." Jake turned and walked toward the meeting room.

"Call me!" Tim's voice faded in the ambient noise.

Jake pushed through the thickening crowd toward the door. A flash of light on the corridor wall caught his eye. He looked up at a silenced TV mounted on the wall. A missing person news story. The image of the young woman stunned Jake. It wasn't that the photo looked like a professional model shot or that she was remarkably beautiful. It was because he knew her. It had been a long time since he'd seen her.

His niece's face was unmistakable.

TWO

Monday, March 22

Jake skipped the panel session and rushed to his hotel room to check the news bulletin he glimpsed on the monitors in the conference center hallway. He opened his laptop and searched for news of Meghan. He clicked on a link to a video report from a local news website.

The video began with a professionally dressed anchorwoman sitting behind a news desk with a photo of Meghan in the background.

"We have breaking news on the disappearance of Meghan Harper, a twenty-year-old student from Stanford University, reported missing by her roommate two weeks ago. Newly obtained surveillance photos show she was last seen at the San Jose Airport returning from Los Angeles." The video flashed with several images of Meghan in casual clothing. One showed her leaving the gate area, one descending the escalators, and another standing in the baggage claim area with her phone in hand. The last one caught Jake's attention; it differed from the others.

The final photo showed her exiting the terminal building wearing a short, tight-fitting dress. She changed clothes? Why would she change into a flirty dress before leaving the airport? Was she going on a date?

"According to police reports, she texted her roommate from the airport saying she was returning home. Instead, she got into a Ride-On rideshare vehicle. Ride-On records showed she went to a park-and-ride lot near Crystal Springs Reservoir, 35 miles from the airport and ten miles from her Palo Alto apartment."

Jake clicked on a video link from the Palo Alto Police Department. Stacey Chaplin, chief of police, stood behind a podium loaded with microphones from the local TV news stations.

"We are treating the disappearance of Meghan Harper as a missing person case. We have no evidence a crime has occurred. However, we are searching for her and interviewing witnesses. Her cell phone is off and we are trying to locate the driver of the rideshare she took the night of March 7. We are asking for the public's help to locate her. Please contact us if you have any information."

Jake searched for articles or videos of statements from Meghan's parents. As expected, he found nothing. Katherine always managed things quietly, privately. At least that's the way she was before cutting ties with him.

Jake's estranged sister, Katherine, was a perfectionist. Image and reputation were the most important things to her; that's what drove a wedge between them. Jake watched Katherine raise her daughter the same way they were raised, the main reason he left home as soon as he became an adult. He loved his niece and recalled a fond, early memory, years before "The Argument."

Katherine entered her pristine living room to find her brother and rambunctious four-year-old roughhousing. "Meghan, time for bed," she groaned as she saw her brother on the floor.

"Come on, Sis. We just got started." Jake on all fours with Meghan on his back, both fists clutching his shirt, bucked and twisted like a mechanical bull in a Western bar.

"More, Uncle Jake!" Meghan squealed; her eyes shut tight.

"That's enough, Jake. You've got her so wound up, she'll never fall asleep." Katherine stood over them with her arms crossed.

"Yee-haw!" Jake bucked upward, sending Meghan flying off, landing with a thud on the freshly vacuumed carpet, bumping a Victorian table, causing the Fernagh-laced lamp on it to tip.

Meghan popped up and clamored back onto her bronco. "More!" She slapped his back like a rodeo cowboy.

Katherine straightened the lamp and smoothed the doily underneath. She scowled at her brother. "That's enough! Jake, stop it!" Katherine's voice rattled the walls.

Jake was all too familiar with her command, one she used since they were kids. He had broken one of Katherine's cardinal rules and knew the consequences if he didn't comply. He stopped bucking and collapsed on the floor as if he'd been shot. "Meghan. Your mom is right. It's time for bed."

"Aww! Uncle Jake." Meghan pouted as she climbed off her mighty steed.

Jake gave Meghan a kiss on her head. Katherine took her hand and led her from the room. Jake waved to Meghan as she disappeared down the hall.

The next morning, Jake drove north from his San Jose hotel. Thirty minutes later, he pulled into a public parking garage in downtown Palo Alto and walked four blocks past city hall and the central fire station. He turned the corner, the main library across the street, the Palo Alto Police Department was half-a-block down.

Jake strode under the arch with "POLICE" in raised block letters above the main entrance, and pushed through the doors of the building. He presented himself to the dark-blue-uniformed receptionist behind an enormous mahogany desk. The brunette with her hair tied back looked up and greeted him.

"How may I help you, sir?" She flashed a warm smile.

Jake returned the smile. "I'm Jake Granger and I'd like to speak to the detective in charge of the Meghan Harper missing person case."

The receptionist typed on her keyboard and read the monitor. "That would be Detective Martinez. May I ask what you would like to speak to him about?"

"I'd like to get some information about the case. I'm Meghan's uncle and I'd like to know what is going on with the investigation."

She eyed him for a moment. "I understand. I'll notify Detective Martinez. If you would like to take a seat, it will be just a few minutes." She pointed to a row of plastic seats lining the wall to Jake's right as she picked up the phone.

Jake sat down and watched plain-clothes and uniformed men and women walk back and forth across the lobby.

The news articles didn't mention the lead investigator by name. Instead, they said, "the police" or "investigators." Martinez. A common surname in California. Jake knew a man named Martinez a long time ago; he wanted to be a cop. Was it the same guy? A bitter taste formed in his mouth. Jake shook his head; the odds were too long. There were probably dozens of detectives named Martinez. It couldn't be the same guy.

The answer appeared through the double doors as they opened to the lobby. He looked a little older, with streaks of gray through a thick forest of black hair and wrinkles around his dark brown eyes. Jake begrudgingly admired his beard and moustache, full and distinguished. He wore a serious look, like a stereotypical TV cop about to interrogate a suspect.

A mixture of anger and disgust flowed through Jake as his former rival crossed the lobby floor. Bitter memories of a battle they waged years ago resurfaced. Could Jake bury his animosity toward Martinez to get the information he came for? How would Martinez react?

For five tense seconds, they faced off like a pair of heavyweights meeting in the center of the ring just before the opening bell. Jake was a couple inches taller. Looking down at the detective eased his apprehension. Martinez extended his hand. A knot grew in Jake's gut. Martinez had a firm grip — one pump and released.

"I never thought I'd see you again." Martinez's glare fixed on Jake's face.

Jake stared back, examining his facial expressions, reading him. "It's a small world. You never know who you'll run into." Jake locked eyes with Martinez like a visual game of chicken. Blink first and lose.

Martinez harrumphed. "You wanted to know about the Meghan Harper case. Follow me." He turned to the double doors and led the way into the inner offices.

The open office space with desks scattered throughout bustled with activity: an elderly man complained about noise from his neighbor's dog, a woman described the man that stole her purse at the mall, a teenager slumped in a chair next to a desk as a detective typed on his computer. The conversations from the surrounding phone calls melded together into a cacophony of voices.

Martinez sat in his chair behind his desk; a laptop lay open in front of him. Jake sat across the desk cluttered with papers and folders. A gold-framed eight-by-ten-inch studio portrait sat prominently next to the computer — Martinez standing next to a stunning brunette holding a young boy in her arms, the picture of the perfect family.

Jake pointed at the picture frame. "Nice family. Cute kid."

"I put that there as a reminder why I come to work every day. My wife, Sylvia, and that's Marco; he's five now. Smart kid."

Jake noticed the designer dress and gold necklace Sylvia wore in the photo. High-maintenance wife. Growing kid. High-rent region. "It must be tough to raise a family on a cop's salary."

Martinez wrinkled his forehead. "We get by. I'm attending law school. Shooting for the DA's office someday."

Jake nodded. Same ambitious guy he knew from the past. If that guy wanted something, he went for it. Jake gnashed his teeth. He didn't want to delve into Martinez's personal life for fear of unearthing old wounds and redirected the conversation back to business. "Meghan?"

"You're her uncle? Your sister's kid?" Martinez glanced at a photo of Meghan on his desk. "I guess there is a family resemblance."

"Yeah, my older sister, Katherine's daughter. Have you spoken to her?"

Martinez screwed his face. "I've spoken to her over the phone. She didn't have much to say. She referred me to her man... Jeeves?"

"Jameson," Jake corrected.

"Yeah. Jameson. He happened to be in the area, so I met with him in person. Have you met him? Strange guy..."

"I met him a couple of times, years ago. Katherine hired him when Meghan was a kid."

Jameson Friedrichs was Katherine's personal secretary and lately had served as her public relations manager. Charles, Katherine's husband, connected with Jameson through one of his California business associates.

Jameson, an ex-highway patrol officer, had good instincts. He could read people, detect frauds and liars. That ability served him well and put him in an excellent position to help Katherine with her affairs. Those skills coupled with his muscular physique made him ideal for the job. No one dared spar with him mentally or physically. He dealt with many weighty issues; dealing with the press and the police were among his tougher duties.

"I guess as their PR guy, he was more concerned with keeping a lid on the details of the case. It sounds like your sister and her husband are big-shots in Denver. They didn't want stuff leaking out to the media. Are you replacing him in some capacity?"

"No. I just learned about Meghan's disappearance and I'm concerned."

"We've been at this for two weeks and we have no leads and no indication your niece is in any danger." He wagged his finger at Jake. "There are volunteer search parties out there looking for her and they haven't come up with anything either. The tip hotline isn't even getting any crackpot leads any more. No sightings of her in New York City or Paris. No clothing found in Tahoe. Not even a friend of a friend of a second cousin reporting her living in a shack in Arizona. We have nothing and it isn't because we haven't been trying."

"What do you think happened to her?"

"I've seen plenty of cases like this. Sure, the media plays up the cases where women disappear and end up dead in a shallow grave somewhere in the woods. What they don't cover are all the cases where the missing person simply ran away from their life, their family. Some of them just got tired of living the life they were living and escaped, disappeared. They dump this life to start over, a new beginning. Dump all the baggage. Forget their past."

That didn't sound like the sweet Meghan Jake knew, but she'd grown up, changed. "Does Meghan fit the profile of someone who would want to just leave her cushy life? Her parents are rich. She's going to one of the best schools in the world. She sounds like she has lots of friends who care about her. How does leaving all that behind make any sense?"

"Meghan is the perfect example of the spoiled little Miss Princess. She's all perfect and cute on the outside, but hidden deep inside is a wild woman itching to bust out. Her parents are loaded, and they have received no ransom demands…"

"No ransom? Are you sure? Like you said, Katherine and Charles have money. It would be a logical motive."

"Do you think your sister would withhold that from us?"

"Maybe."

"It's been two weeks. Kidnappers would want their money quick, so no, I don't think there has been any ransom demands, but your sister's holding something back; I can smell it. They won't even make any public appeals. Jameson told me they are private people. Does that sound like your sister?"

Jake shook his head. "I haven't spoken to her in a long time, but I'm not surprised by her reaction. I want to make sure Meghan's case is taken seriously."

Martinez's jaw tightened. Veins bulged in his neck. His eyes narrowed and nostrils flared. "We take every report seriously, especially when it involves young women that disappear in the night. What do you really want?"

Martinez rose from his seat, glaring at Jake. Jake stood to meet his eyes. They leaned toward each other like a pair of rams ready to butt heads on a mountainside.

"This is about what happened between me and Samantha, isn't it?" Martinez glanced around at the other detectives in the area engaged in their own conversations. "You really don't give a shit about this case. You just saw a chance to stick it to me. Maybe call my lieutenant and file a complaint? Is that what this is all about?"

"Yes, I'm still pissed at you for fucking my fiancée. But I came here to find out what you are doing to find my niece," Jake hissed.

Jake and Martinez had been friends while they served in the Army stationed in Langley, Virginia. Samantha worked in IT in the same building. The three of them socialized together, and the trio formed a strong friendship. Jake and Samantha struck up a romantic relationship, and he proposed to her after a year-long courtship.

One evening after too much drinking by all parties, Samantha and Martinez found themselves together alone. In the heat of drunken passion, they had sex. The next morning, Samantha confessed her indiscretion to Jake. He forgave her, but exploded on Martinez. It took months before they spoke to each other; that was nineteen years ago.

"It was a mistake. A big mistake. I apologized for that years ago, and so did Samantha. You have got to let it go," Martinez whispered. "You wanted information about Meghan's case. Do you want my help or not?"

Jake glanced around the room and noticed the other detectives staring at them. Jake put his hands up as if surrendering and sank down into his seat. "OK. What have you got?" Jake asked.

Martinez sighed. "This is an active investigation, so I can't tell you anything more than you could probably find in the newspapers."

"I've read the articles. What else can you tell me?"

Martinez opened his notebook and thumbed to the page of notes concerning Meghan's disappearance. He read the facts of the case in a staccato tempo like he was Sergeant Joe Friday from the old TV show, *Dragnet*. "Airport surveillance video shows she arrived in San Jose on March 7 at 11:00 PM. She texted her roommate at 11:05. She ordered a rideshare that picked her up at 11:33 PM and dropped her off at her assigned destination at 12:11 AM, a park-and-ride lot at the intersection of State Route 92 and Interstate 280 near the Crystal Springs Reservoir."

"Have you located the rideshare driver?"

"No." Martinez hesitated. "We don't think he's involved with her disappearance."

"Really? Why not?"

"Ride-On's records indicate he picked up other riders immediately after he dropped off your niece at Crystal Springs."

Jake wasn't going to argue with Martinez over how many ways there were to tamper with the ridesharing company's database records to make it look like the driver picked up other riders that night.

"You don't think it's suspicious that the driver disappeared the same time as Meghan?"

"He's not a person of interest. We have no reason to pursue that avenue. We don't even know if a crime has been committed," Martinez replied with a tinge of irritation in his voice. Jake opened his mouth, but Martinez stopped him with an index finger pointed up. "Before you ask, we have not released the name of the driver. Again, because he's not a person of interest. There is no need to put his name out there unnecessarily."

Jake bristled, not satisfied with the answer. "I think…"

"I really don't care what you think." Martinez gave Jake an icy glare. "I know that look in your eye. I know you want to go off half-cocked searching for that guy. You haven't changed a bit. I'm warning you. Don't start your own investigation. This is police business. We follow procedures to make sure our case sticks in court. Let us do our jobs." Martinez glanced around the room at his cohorts and anyone else within earshot, and leaned toward Jake. "Your sister's man, Jameson, told me this wasn't the first time Meghan had run away. He assured me there was nothing to be concerned about."

"And you believed that?" Jake shot back.

Martinez shrugged. "Her parents aren't concerned, so why are you?"

There was no point in discussing this with Martinez any further. There was also no point in following the detective's orders. The rideshare driver was the last one to see Meghan. Were the Ride-On records accurate? Did he really pick up other riders immediately after dropping off Meghan near the reservoir? Or did he have time to take her somewhere? Jake changed the subject.

"What did the roommate say? What's her name?"

"I'm not at liberty to reveal the roommate's name. Privacy, you know. She had nothing else to say to us, but she acted suspicious to me."

"Suspicious? How?"

"I think she's holding out on us, too. She's covering for her."

"Wasn't she the one that reported her missing? Why would she do that if she wanted to help Meghan hide?"

Martinez shrugged.

"Has there been any activity on her phone?"

"Nope. Nothing since she was dropped off at the park-and-ride. Her phone is off."

Why would she tell her roommate she was coming home when she ordered a ride elsewhere? Jake needed to learn more about his niece; he had to talk to her roommate.

THREE

Tuesday, March 23

Cooperation was a two-way street. Detective Martinez refused to give Jake any information about Meghan's roommate, so Jake would not heed his warning to stay out of police business. Martinez's refusal to give him any information about Meghan's roommate wouldn't stop Jake. In his business, he had tracked down more elusive people. The Internet contained all the information he needed; it was a matter of sorting through the posts, tweets, and blogs to find the most useful tidbits.

Jake searched online for news articles mentioning Meghan's roommate. One referred to her as Alexis Gray, a junior biology major at Stanford. Jake smirked as he recalled the smug expression Martinez had when he refused to cooperate with him. If they were keeping score, he was ahead 1-0.

Alexis was born in a Chicago suburb to a middle-class couple: her mother a nurse in a community clinic, her father a sales manager for a department store. Her parents scrimped since she was an infant to send her to college. Alexis earned straight-As in high school and won an academic scholarship so she could afford to attend the $70,000-per-year university. Even with her parents' college fund and the scholarship, her finances were tight. Splitting the cost of an apartment with Meghan helped.

Jake clicked the video link showing a blonde, ponytail wagging, stapling a poster with Meghan's picture on it to a telephone pole. A female voice-over narrated.

"Volunteers have been working tirelessly in efforts to develop leads on the disappearance of Meghan Harper, a Stanford student that went missing mysteriously nearly a week ago. Today, we have Meghan's roommate and close friend, Alexis Gray, also a student at Stanford. She was perhaps the last person to hear from Meghan before she disappeared."

The petite woman put down her posters, turned, and faced the camera.

"Alexis. Please tell us what happened." The female reporter shoved a microphone into her face.

Alexis's cheeks sagged. Jake imagined if she smiled, they'd look fuller. Her lips formed a tight red line across her face. Makeup couldn't hide the dark circles under her eyes. She took a deep breath before she spoke.

"Meghan was returning on a flight from LA. I worried about her coming home so late, so I made her promise to text me as soon as she arrived in San Jose. Her text said she had landed and was on her way, but she never came home. I got worried, so I called the cops," Alexis said in a clear, determined voice as if someone had hit the "Play" button on a tape recorder.

The video switched to a selfie of Meghan. Her beaming smile reminded Jake of earlier times with his niece. When he worked in Army Intelligence near Washington, D.C., Jake had visited Katherine and Meghan in their Denver home as often as his schedule allowed. He loved his niece and made the most of his limited time with her. Jake smiled at a memory when Meghan was a child.

Eight-year-old Meghan sat on the piano bench wearing a frilly pink dress, hair pulled back, ruby lipstick, looking like a doll in a department store window display, thanks to Katherine's fastidious efforts. Her tiny fingers rested on the keys, ready to perform. A hush fell over the audience in the church auditorium. Friends of the family, her father's business associates, church and community members, and her parents awaited her performance.

Meghan jiggled her foot. She took a deep breath. She had played this piece a thousand times; she could do it one more time for the people in front of her. A lot was at stake. White-haired Mrs. Whitaker, her private instructor, nodded, and Meghan played.

Meghan read the notes to Beethoven's "Moonlight Sonata" on the pages in front of her but didn't need to. Weeks of preparation and rehearsal paid off. Muscle memory and a sense of oneness with the music flowed through her hands, executing the piece flawlessly. Her fingers caressed the ivory. Her head rocked with Mrs. Whitaker's hand movements, marking the rhythm.

Meghan loved playing; she loved performing in front of audiences. She was skilled and enjoyed showing off, but following the rules, being perfect, looking perfect, took patience and effort. The fruits of her labor showed during her performance.

Near the end of her performance, due to fatigue or a lapse in concentration, a finger slipped, a wrong note struck. A gasp from her mother in the audience. Meghan finished playing to enthusiastic applause from everyone save one.

Backstage after her performance, Meghan waited in the cramped dressing room, bracing for the onslaught that would befall her. It had happened before; it would happen again. The anger. The disappointment.

Katherine stormed in, dismissing all others — outsiders had no right to witness her private reprimands. She slammed the door behind them.

Jake crept to the door, opened it a crack, and peered inside. Entering would have been a disaster.

"What was that?" Katherine screeched at her daughter. "We practiced this over and over. I told you to be careful! Do you know what this means?"

Meghan nodded.

"It means shame. Shame for you. Shame for me. What you do reflects on the whole family. People look up to us."

It was her philosophy. Katherine was a zealot in the religion of reputation and social standing. Image was everything to her. Perfect children came from perfect parents. Perfect parents deserved the admiration and respect of those inferior to them. Katherine craved adoration; she lusted for it. She couldn't live without it — it was her heroin.

"I'm sorry, Mother," Meghan said, head bowed. "I don't know what happened."

"It's because you skip out on practices. Mrs. Whitaker has told me you've missed several practices. Where do you go? What do you do?"

"Nowhere. Sometimes I want to…"

"We'll make sure it doesn't happen again. Practice makes perfect. That's what I was taught by my parents. I'll ask Mrs. Whitaker to spend an extra hour a day with you and I will make sure you stop missing your sessions."

"Yes, Mother," sighed Meghan.

Katherine's posture relaxed: her shoulders drooped, her back bent, she leaned in toward Meghan, and pushed a stray hair from Meghan's face. She whispered, "I'm trying to protect you, don't you see? I want what is best for you. I want you to be the best you can be. You can do better. It's important. When you grow up, you'll understand. For now, just do as I say and everything will be fine; I promise." She wrapped an arm around Meghan's shoulder and squeezed.

"I understand. I won't disappoint you," Meghan said with no confidence in her voice.

Jake sensed it was safe to enter. He rapped on the wooden door and flung it open. "There you are! I've been looking everywhere for you!" He squatted down to be eye-level with his niece. "You were marvelous, dear!" He looked up at his sister. "Isn't that right, Sis?" Katherine glowered and remained silent. He turned back to Meghan. "You deserve a treat. How about some ice cream?" Meghan's face beamed.

"After more practice," Katherine insisted. "It's best to fix the errors right away." She motioned for Meghan to leave. "Find Mrs. Whitaker and tell her you want to practice more."

Practice makes perfect. The mantra stuck with Katherine, less so with Jake. It took the United States Army boot camp to drive discipline into him.

When Meghan left the room, Katherine said to Jake, "It's not good to coddle her like that. Did you hear her mistake?"

"It was one note. What's the harm? She's just a child. You'll give her some kind of complex if you keep putting that kind of pressure on her."

"Nonsense. This was the way our parents raised me, and this is how I will raise my child. Children grow up. Flawed children grow up flawed. I will do whatever necessary to ensure she reaches her full potential. I know what's best for my daughter and she will do as I say."

Jake shook his head. "I hope you know what you're doing."

"I do." Katherine stalked away to observe and critique Meghan's post-recital practice.

The video returned to the reporter speaking to Alexis, awaking Jake from his trance.

"I see you're putting up posters. What else are you doing to find your friend?" the reporter asked.

"The police are doing their investigation. Meghan's friends and I have gone online and put out information on all the social media platforms. We've formed search parties to follow up on leads. We're doing everything we can to spread the word." Alexis turned to face the camera, tears welling in her eyes.

The reporter wrapped her arm around Alexis's shoulders. "You are working hard to find your friend. You must care about her."

"I've known Meghan since we were freshmen. I miss her. I want her to come home." Alexis wiped the tears from her eyes. "If anyone knows anything about where she is, please contact us or the police." Alexis clasped her hands in front of her face.

Jake hadn't seen or spoken to Meghan in years; the child he used to carry on his back had grown up; he didn't know his niece anymore, but her roommate did. Jake needed to talk to Alexis.

Under normal circumstances, the quickest way for Jake to find Alexis would be to call his sister, Katherine, and ask for Meghan's address; but that wasn't an option he wanted to exercise. He wasn't sure she'd tell him, even if he could muster the courage to contact her. He opted to rely on the methods he used at work to locate Alexis.

Jake searched online directories and found an address. Meghan and Alexis lived in a Palo Alto apartment — in the high-rent district; as if there was a low-rent district in Palo Alto, one of the priciest zip codes in the state. Meghan's parents made sure she lived in the lap of luxury. How could Alexis afford her half of the rent?

A canopy of hundred-year-old oaks arched over the street leading to Alexis and Meghan's apartment. Lush, well-manicured lawns, bushes trimmed into animal topiaries, polished late-model cars and SUVs parked in the driveways. The neighborhood, a picture out of *Better Homes and Gardens*.

Jake drove to the four-story apartment complex, nestled amongst old-growth oak trees surrounding the property. He parked his car in a visitor's slot and checked the mailboxes for the unit number. He climbed the exterior stairs to the fourth floor, circled the concrete walkway, stopped in front of the door marked 415, and knocked.

Bare feet slapped the tile on the other side of the door.

"Who is it?" a female voice called through the closed door. "If you are the press, I don't want to talk. I'm all talked out."

"Alexis Gray? I'm not with the press. My name is Jake Granger. I'm Meghan's uncle."

The door eased open revealing Alexis, her hair a tousled mane and wearing a rumpled t-shirt and shorts. Her eyes drooped like she'd just woke up.

"Uncle Jake!" Alexis flung her arms around his neck, stood tiptoe, and hugged him tight around the neck.

The sudden embrace surprised him. He took a staggering step forward to maintain his balance.

She dropped, feet slapping the floor, and took him by the hand. "I'm sorry I startled you. It's just that Meghan has told me so much about you. I hope you don't mind that I call you Uncle Jake. Through the stories she's told me, I feel like I know you." She closed the door and led him to the living room.

Fashion magazines covered the coffee table. A knitted, multi-colored blanket hung across the couch. She kicked aside soiled clothing on the floor and picked up the blanket. "Please have a seat. I'm so glad to meet you."

"It's nice to meet you. I have to say, I didn't expect that greeting," Jake said as he lowered himself to the couch.

"Meghan said she always had fun when you came to visit her. She had lots of fond memories." Alexis sat down cross-legged facing him. She dropped her chin. "I guess you're here because of her."

"That's right. I just spoke to Detective Martinez…"

Alexis shot up and paced the floor; her feet pounded the carpet. Through gritted teeth, she said, "The cops are useless. They made it sound like she'd run away. They think she's hiding." Alexis stopped pacing and plopped down on the couch next to Jake. "I'm sorry, but that cop, Detective Martinez, such a pompous ass. It makes me mad just thinking about him and his smug grin. I don't trust him. Mr. Know-It-All. He said he'd seen cases like this before. A person disappears because they're tired of their dull, routine lives and run away from it all. That's bullshit. Meghan was happy, active. She wouldn't just run away, especially after telling me she was on her way home."

Jake kept his face stern, but smiled within. Someone who agreed with him about Martinez, an ally.

"Do you think something bad has happened to her?"

"Yes! Do you think I'd be this upset if I didn't?" She waved her arms in the air.

Jake's eyebrows flew up at the passionate response. Alexis was one of those people who let their emotions show quickly. "Why do you think she's in trouble?"

"You sound like a cop." Alexis pursed her lips.

"Maybe, but help me understand. Is she involved in something?"

Alexis's eyes bored in on his. She planted her fists on her hips. "No! She's a good girl. She's no different from anyone else. She did nothing wrong!" She stomped her foot, rattling the window.

The volatile reaction startled Jake. Was her reaction genuine? Or was she putting on a show for him?

"I don't want them to find Meghan dead in a shallow grave in the middle of nowhere like some cases I've read," Alexis continued. "We have to find her."

Jake recalled a news story from three months earlier about a female college student who disappeared after a party. Searchers found her body weeks later at the bottom of a lake. They arrested the woman's boyfriend, who confessed to the crime.

"Meghan probably told you we hadn't spoken in a long time," Jake began. Alexis nodded. She thankfully didn't press for an explanation. He didn't want to get into that sordid tale. "What does Meghan like to do these days?"

"Normal stuff. She's the outdoorsy type. Hiking. Skiing. And of course, studying."

"What's she studying?"

"She's a chem major, so she spends a lot of time in the lab, sometimes late at night running experiments or studying in the library."

"What about her social life?"

"What about it?" Alexis answered his question with a question, looking at her feet, avoiding eye contact.

Suspicion gnawed at Jake's gut; alarm bells rang in his head. He'd interviewed too many suspected hackers to miss the signs. She was hiding something. "Does she go out?"

"You mean like on dates?" Again, answering his question with a question.

"Yeah, on dates."

"Sure. Everybody dates. Like I said, she's a normal girl. She does normal girl stuff. We'd get together once in a while with friends." Alexis frowned at him like he had offended her lifestyle. "Anyone should be able to have some fun every once in a while."

Jake's internal lie detector wasn't detecting a lie, but Alexis was being evasive. "I agree she should have fun, but was she seeing anyone in particular? Was there anyone special in her life?"

"No!" Alexis spat. "No one special."

Jake noted the way she emphasized the word "special" but didn't press her on it. "What else can you tell me about her?"

"She wouldn't just disappear like this. She's super-reliable. If she promised something, she'd do it no matter what. She kept her word. That's why when she told me she was coming home and didn't, I knew something had happened to her. If she had a change in plans, she'd have told me." Alexis re-established eye contact.

Alexis seemed more at ease talking about this part of Meghan's character, but it wasn't giving him any clues about where Meghan might be. "Had she been in any fights or arguments with anyone?"

"No. Everyone loves Meghan. She has lots of friends. She is the kindest and most generous person. She helps at the Palo Alto Community Outreach Center to help the homeless and abused women. She's a wonderful friend. If you need anything, she's there for you."

Alexis explained all the things Meghan's friends did to help search for her. Unfortunately, as time wore on, the number of volunteers waned and the media lost interest, chasing the next big story elsewhere. A gangland shoot-out in Oakland, a hit-and-run involving a mother and child, a protest against climate change, and the drug problem in homeless encampments stole the headlines. Public interest in finding Meghan dwindled.

"The police said the rideshare driver was the last one to see Meghan. Martinez can't or won't go looking for him and he won't tell me his name or his address, but I think he's the key to finding Meghan."

"What else can we do?" Alexis asked.

"We'll find him on our own, but I'll need your help."

FOUR

Tuesday, March 23

The Ride-On driver saw her last; he took her to a remote spot in San Mateo County. According to Alexis, Meghan had no reason to go there. Did she meet someone? Where did she go? The rideshare company records showed the driver had an alibi. Could he have tampered with the Ride-On database? To find the answers, Jake had to find the driver.

Jake needed the driver's name and home address. The police didn't release any personal information about the driver to the public or the media, and Martinez didn't reveal any clues to Jake. He'd have to find another way.

"Do you have a computer we can use?" Jake asked Alexis.

"Sure." Alexis scurried into her bedroom and returned with a silver laptop, placed it on the coffee table, and opened the lid. "Now what? Meghan told me you are some kind of computer expert. Are you going to hack the rideshare computers?" Alexis pulled up a chair and sat down next to Jake, eyes wide, licking her lips. "I've always wanted to see a hacker work."

"I don't think I have to. There's a quicker way. I just need to get into Meghan's account — with your help."

Alexis pouted and frowned. "My help? What can I do?"

"Pretend to be Meghan."

Alexis shook her head. The furrows in her brow deepened. "Pretend to be Meghan?" she repeated.

Jake opened a web browser on the laptop and entered the URL for the rideshare company. He clicked on the "Help" button on the web page and located the helpdesk phone number. He pulled out his phone. "Tell them you've lost your phone and you don't remember your login information. Plead with them. Tell them it's an emergency. Act flustered and confused. If they ask you for Meghan's personal information, tell them you can't remember."

Jake had seen how she pleaded for help on TV. He experienced first-hand how dramatic she could be. He was convinced she could lie.

"I can't do that! They won't believe me. They won't just give me her login information without proof."

"Trust me. Give them a sob story. People are basically helpful, even helpdesk people. Prey on that. Sound pitiful. They will break protocol in an emergency. Sound desperate. Really sell it."

"I don't know if I can."

Jake smiled. "Have you ever acted in a play? High school, perhaps?"

Alexis grinned. "Yes. *Kiss Me Kate*. I played the part of Lois Lane. I was pretty good"

"Lois Lane! It's funny how that character's name is the same as Superman's girlfriend." Jake guffawed. Alexis shook her head at his nerdy reference. "I'm sure you were fantastic. Just channel your inner Lois Lane on this call, and you'll be fine."

Alexis sighed, "OK, I'll try. Give me a second." She closed her eyes, inhaled deeply, and exhaled loudly. She opened her eyes and said, "I'm ready."

Jake dialed the number for the Ride-On helpdesk. "Remember, sound desperate." He handed her the phone.

Jake listened in as Alexis put on an Oscar-winning performance. She convinced the online support representative she was Meghan and had lost her phone, which had her login information. She was away from home and desperately needed to post an announcement on the website to her friends and relatives about an unspecified personal emergency. She needed to do it before people got on airplanes unnecessarily. She cried. She pleaded. The tone in her voice was heart-breaking.

The young-sounding man assured her he would do everything he could to help her. After a minute of typing, he said, "We're all set. I'll email you your username and password."

Jake shook his head and pointed to the phone.

"No! I don't have access to my email either. Please, can you give me that information now, over the phone?" Alexis mixed charm and pitifulness in her voice like a ten-year-old pleading for another scoop of ice cream for dessert. "I will forever be in your debt." Her voice like honey, sweet and smooth.

Silence on the line.

"OK," the rep said. He gave Alexis Meghan's username and a temporary password. "Please change the password as soon as you successfully log in."

Alexis scribbled the login credentials on a piece of scrap paper, thanked the gullible man profusely, and ended the call. She slumped in her seat. "Whew! He fell for that act."

"That was an impressive performance."

"Maybe I missed my calling." Alexis handed Jake the piece of paper. "Now what?"

"Now we check her ride history."

Jake logged into the Ride-On website using Meghan's credentials and reviewed her ride records. Her last entries were: Picked up by Naadir Abdullah on March 7 at 11:33 PM and dropped off at 12:11 AM on the 8th.

"The driver's name was Naadir Abdullah. Next, we have to find out where he lives."

Alexis rubbed her hands together. "Now, are you going to hack their computer to get his address?" She scooted her chair closer to Jake's.

Alexis was cavalier about circumventing the rideshare company's network and computer defenses. She didn't understand the complexities of such a task. Cop and spy movies made it seem simple and quick to subvert cyber defenses; reality was more complex.

Computers and networks had vulnerabilities, weaknesses that could be exploited. All organizations conduct risk analyses — a cost-benefit analysis. Budget, time, and manpower constraints dictated how much to invest in security measures. Unfortunately, given enough time and effort, an experienced, determined hacker could breach those defenses.

While there were thousands of computer security professionals roaming the halls at the CyberSec Conference, only a few dozen had the skills to defeat the security measures Ride-On had implemented to protect their users' data. Jake was one of them; that's what made his skills so valuable. Even with his skills, hacking corporate servers took time.

Jake came to California to attend the CyberSec Conference and schmooze with potential clients. The conference was into its second day. He lamented the missed opportunities to win some consulting deals and make some money. But finding Meghan was the priority. He first had to locate Naadir Abdullah, and he didn't have time to hack the Ride-on servers.

"I have a better idea."

"What are you going to do?"

"I'm going to find Abdullah's address the same way I found yours. I'm going to do an Internet search on his name and see what we can find."

"You found my address on the Internet without hacking? You just googled it?" Alexis narrowed her eyes and curled her lips.

"You'd be amazed at what you can find with the right kind of searches."

"I feel exposed. I thought I was safe. If you could find me, so could..." She clamped her lips and crossed her arms.

Jake typed Naadir's name in the search engine and scrolled through the results. He stopped on two entries in an online address directory. "Here are two locals. Let's see where they are on the map." He opened a new browser tab to a map search site and entered the first address. He zoomed in on the San Jose address and frowned.

"What is it?"

"This address is...." Jake clicked the keys and mouse like crickets in summer. He stopped and leaned back in his chair. "This is a nursing home. This guy is a senior citizen. There is no way he's a rideshare driver."

"It must be this other guy. He lives in Palo Alto." Alexis pointed to the other address.

Jake pulled up a map of the new location.

Alexis stated at the monitor. "I know that place. It's an on-campus apartment complex for grad students."

"Grad student? Let's see what else we can find out about this Naadir." Jake continued typing.

After five minutes of searching, Jake said, "There are results for a chemistry grad student at Stanford."

"Chem student? At Stanford? Do you think Meghan knew him?" Alexis leaned into the screen to read the articles about Naadir's background on the Stanford website.

"He's also the local president of the Muslim American Coalition of California. He seems to be quite active in that organization." Jake pointed to articles quoting Naadir.

"Are you going to his apartment?"

Jake followed a link on a search result, an announcement for a Coalition event. "There's a rally going on right now in Sunnyvale. Maybe I can find him there."

Jake dashed out the door without saying goodbye to Alexis.

An ethnically diverse group of a hundred people gathered at Sunnyvale's Central Park under the warm midday sun around a makeshift wooden platform. Loudspeakers blared music as the presenters prepared to address the crowd. Jake joined the curious onlookers along the perimeter.

The music stopped. A bearded man in his twenties spoke into the microphone; his voice boomed through the speakers. "Good afternoon and on behalf of the Muslim American Coalition, I welcome you to our rally to create awareness to the offenses of this government against those of the Muslim faith. I am Naadir Abdullah, president of the California chapter of our organization."

Naadir wasn't hiding. He was out in the open, prominent, speaking at rallies in public parks. Why couldn't Martinez and the Palo Alto Police Department find him? Did Martinez lie about this?

Naadir continued his fifteen-minute speech before introducing the next speaker. Jake meandered closer to the stage as the various speakers presented their thoughts and shared their experiences. Jake paid no attention to what they were saying; he kept his focus on Naadir, standing to the right of the stage.

An hour into the rally, a Sunnyvale Safety patrol car stopped along the street near the gathering. A pair of uniformed officers emerged and walked toward the orderly group. Pistol holsters slapped their thighs and handcuffs clinked on their belts as they approached.

Naadir spotted the approaching officers and intercepted them.

"What seems to be the problem, officer?"

The officer with sergeant stripes on his shoulder replied, "We received a complaint from one of the neighbors. Do you have a permit for this gathering?"

"Permit? No. I didn't think we needed a permit."

Four men in their twenties and thirties broke from the crowd, rushing toward Naadir and the officers.

Naadir held up his hand to the men. "It's cool. There is no need for a confrontation. We needed a permit. It was my oversight. We'll leave, officers." He stepped onto the platform and spoke into the microphone, "I'm very sorry, but we will need to conclude this rally. Thank you all for attending. Please check our website for our next event." He motioned to his crew to dismantle the audio equipment.

The crowd dispersed, murmuring. The police officers walked back toward their cruiser.

Jake saw his opportunity and jumped in front of Naadir, startling him.

"Do you know where Meghan Harper is?"

Half-a-dozen of Naadir's associates noticed the stranger standing nose-to-nose with their leader and closed in.

"Who? Who are you?" Naadir leaned away from Jake.

"Naadir! Are you OK? Is this man bothering you?" a tall man wearing khaki pants asked.

"I'm fine," Naadir replied to his friend. He said to Jake, "I don't know anyone named Meghan… Wait! Meghan Harper? The missing woman? I heard about her through the campus news." He frowned at Jake. "Do you think I had something to do with her disappearance?"

The tall man shoved Jake away from Naadir. Reflexes kicked in and Jake shoved back. In an instant, three other men pounced on Jake, pinning him to the ground.

"You were her rideshare driver. Tell me where Meghan is! Where did you take her?" Jake yelled as he twisted to break free.

The officers heard the commotion, turned around, and raced toward the agitated group of men.

"Break it up!" ordered the sergeant. He and his partner pulled the men off Jake.

"Tell me where she is!" Jake lunged at Naadir.

The sergeant grabbed Jake's arm and twisted it behind his back. His partner grabbed his other arm and pushed him face-down into the grass. "Cuff him!"

FIVE

Wednesday, March 24

One good thing about being arrested in Sunnyvale was Jake didn't have to face Martinez. Did the two police departments share their arrest information? Would Martinez eventually find out?

Naadir Abdullah declined to press assault charges against Jake, and the two police officers chose not to charge him with causing a public nuisance and resisting arrest. The police released him after a couple of hours in a holding room at the Sunnyvale Safety offices.

Jake returned to his hotel room to continue his investigation. Upon deeper examination, Jake uncovered articles showing Naadir Abdullah was in Washington, D.C. on March 7 delivering a speech at a Muslim American Coalition event to a group of three hundred politicians and business leaders. Jake had the wrong guy.

Maybe Alexis was right. Hacking the Ride-On database might be the quickest way to find Naadir? The Palo Alto police had access to the database; they had his address, but Martinez said they couldn't find him. Was he lying? Did Jake's internal lie detector fizzle? Was he so angry at Martinez he had missed the signs? If Martinez thought Naadir was involved in Meghan's disappearance, he would search his residence. To search the residence, he'd need a court-ordered search warrant. There would be a record of that warrant. How could he check?

Jake fished out Tim McGuire's business card from his jacket pocket and called the Stockton reporter.

"Tim, are you still interested in interviewing me?"

"Yes, of course. When are you available? It's already Wednesday. Are you leaving right after the conference?"

"I'm not sure when I'm available and I'm not sure when I'm leaving. Things are kind of in flux for me right now, but I promise if you will do me this favor, I'll make every effort to fit you into my schedule."

"Favor? What kind of favor?"

"I have a name. Can you find out if a search warrant was issued to the Palo Alto Police?"

Silence on the line.

"Tim. You there? Did you hear me?"

"That is a strange request. Why do you need to…"

"Never mind why. Do we have a deal?"

Jake drove across town to the Evergreen district of San Jose. Abutting the sandstone hillside with Mount Hamilton topping the range, the residential neighborhood had a mixture of neat 1950s ranchers and newly rebuilt two-story homes, each costing close to a million dollars in the supernova-hot Silicon Valley housing market. The streets were clean and devoid of cars after the commuter rush, a sign of a working-class community.

Jake exited the expressway, passing apartment complexes and strip malls. The signs over the businesses reflected the ethnic diversity of the neighborhood: an Indian restaurant, a Muslim mosque, an Asian hairstylist. Jake's GPS guided him through a maze of roads, past parks and schools. Energetic children played in school yards; young mothers pushed baby strollers along sidewalks. Jake made the final turn up a hill and his GPS app announced his arrival at his destination.

Tim McGuire came through. He confirmed the Palo Alto Police Department executed a search warrant for Naadir Abdullah, a forty-five-year-old Afghan immigrant at his San Jose residence. He gave Jake the address.

Naadir's home looked like many Jake had seen in the neighborhood, a single-story tan stucco-clad house with a dark brown shingle roof. The two-car garage stuck out in front of the rest of the structure with an older model white Honda Civic parked in the driveway. The lawn needed a trim.

He strode to the front door, noting the quiet of his surroundings. He pressed the doorbell; a chime sounded inside. No answer. He waited five seconds and knocked on the door. No response, knocked again, a rustling within. He peeked through the living room window next to the door; a shadow passed along the floor.

"Mrs. Abdullah! Hello! My name is Jake Granger. I'd like to talk to you about your husband," Jake yelled at the door. He pounded on the door. "Mrs. Abdullah? Are you in there?"

Jake pressed his ear against the door. Footsteps approached; he took a step back. The door cracked open.

A dark-haired woman with intense green eyes peeked from around the door. She spoke in a language he hadn't heard in over two decades. "Go away! I do not know where my husband is." She slammed the door.

Jake had learned Pashto during his tours in Afghanistan with Army Intelligence. Even when he lived there, his speaking skills in that language were barely passable. He could order food at the local restaurants and ask for directions. Those rudimentary sentences would not go far in helping him communicate with a woman whose husband was missing. He empathized with her, but he needed her help.

"Mrs. Abdullah, please," Jake croaked in broken Pashto. Foreign languages weren't his strengths. He hoped he pronounced the word for "please" correctly. The natives in Afghanistan constantly criticized his inability to pronounce words properly in their native tongue. Immigrants, especially those from the Middle East, distrusted the U.S. immigration agencies, making her suspicious of strangers. He sensed her near the other side of the door. "I'm not with the police or the government. I know they have been a nuisance to you." Jake had learned the word for "nuisance" from a beautiful woman in Kabul who didn't appreciate his advances. "I'm a friend of the... a friend of Meghan, the missing woman. Could I speak to you? Please?"

The door creaked open. She stared at him, examining his face. After a moment, she lowered her eyes and opened the door wide.

Jake entered the neat home decorated with a mixture of modern American furnishings: overstuffed sofa and big-screen TV, and traditional Afghan appointments: an area carpet and several intricate vases. He sat on the sofa; Mrs. Abdullah, in her recliner.

Jake explained in his limited Pashto why he was there, his relationship to Meghan, and his desire to find out what happened to her. Mrs. Abdullah listened intently, but remained silent. Jake wasn't sure if she was quiet because she was thinking or because she hadn't understood a word he had said.

Finally, she said in English, "My husband left for work one day and didn't return. The police said that was the day after the woman disappeared. They frightened me."

Jake sighed in relief as he replied in English. "I'm very sorry."

"This has been a terrible experience for me and my children. The police came and questioned me. They took my husband's things. I am glad the police have gone. I am scared."

"I understand…"

"The government took my friends' and neighbors' husbands away. They don't know why. Or where their husbands are. I wish for my husband's safe return. I wish for this nightmare to end."

"I would like to help," Jake said.

"I don't trust the police. I don't trust your government."

"I don't blame you. I just want to find Meghan. I don't believe your husband was involved, but I'm sure he knows something that can help me find her."

She studied his face. "You remind me of an American I met in Kabul. He had kind eyes like yours. He helped us come to America. Can I trust you?"

"Yes, you can trust me. Did you say your husband went to work? Where does he work?"

"He works at an automobile repair shop a few miles from here. The American I told you about helped my husband get that job." She handed Jake a business card with the name and address of the shop.

Jake examined the card and asked, "Did you tell the police this?"

"I didn't have to. They knew and already checked there."

Jake slipped the card into his shirt pocket. "Thank you. I'll pay them a visit."

SIX

Wednesday, March 24

Jake passed warehouses and small manufacturing plants on his way to Bruce's Auto Body Shop, jets overhead, departing from the San Jose Airport, a mile away. He parked on the busy four-lane street. In the driveway in front of the large, open garage door stood a red 1960s vintage Corvette with a dented hood and crunched bumper. How much would it cost the owner to repair that kind or damage on the classic vehicle? On the street, a 1990s Toyota Camry with a scrape stretching the length of the driver's side, deep enough to show streaks of bare sheet metal.

Jake got out of his car and approached the shop; it looked narrow, barely wide enough for three cars to park in front. As he entered the interior, the garage extended a hundred yards back and broadened to accommodate a dozen cars in various stages of repair.

Jake spotted a mechanic, head stuck under the hood of a Ford pickup.

"Excuse me. I'm looking for Bruce," Jake said to the man's back.

The busy repairman pointed toward the back of the garage, but said nothing, keeping his head next to the truck's exhaust manifold.

"Thanks," Jake replied over the squeal of pneumatic wrenches, the hiss of hydraulic lifts, and the clang of metal objects bouncing off the concrete floor. Jake walked to a mechanic looking up at the undercarriage of a raised Buick, a shop lamp in his hand.

"Are you Bruce?" Jake stared at the underside of the car as if he knew anything about auto repair.

"Yeah, who are you?" Bruce replied without taking his eyes off his work.

"Does Naadir Abdullah work for you?" Jake explained to the shop owner why he was there and what he hoped to learn.

Bruce switched off the lamp and set it on a workbench. He crossed his arms and leaned against the bench. "I've already talked to the cops about him. I'll tell you what I told them. He used to work for me. One day he decided not to show up, no warning, so I fired him. Too bad, smart guy; he did outstanding work, but I can't afford to have unreliable workers."

"Do you know where he might be?"

Bruce raised his hands in surrender. "Like I said, he didn't show for work and I have no fucking idea where he is. I got nothing else to say. He worked for me. We didn't hang out together or go out for drinks. I know nothing about him."

"What about the other mechanics? Any of them close to him?"

"I don't think so, but you can ask around. Don't take too much time. We got a butt-ton of work and I'm a man down with Naadir gone."

Jake made the rounds and talked to the other mechanics. None of them had anything but opinions to offer.

Gerald, an Oakland native, thought Naadir might have been dealing drugs on the side because all the people from Afghanistan grew opium and dealt drugs. His brother OD'd on heroin the previous month.

Pete, a Vietnam-era Army vet, didn't talk to Naadir much, just the passing hello, but thought he was a strait-laced guy. Hard-working, unlike Gerald.

Jake met Tammy working in the office.

"Who the fuck are you? Can't you see I'm busy?"

Tammy, Bruce's wife, used the F-word like it was a comma, but after Jake explained why he interrupted her, she cooperated.

She was in the office that morning. It was early, around seven. She usually opened the shop to start her office work. She was at her desk when she heard Naadir's voice. When he didn't appear a few minutes later, she checked but found nothing.

"Where did you hear his voice?" Jake asked.

"Around back. The guys usually enter from the back. The front door is for customers and cars."

Jake walked out the back door and scanned the scene, a dumping ground for scrap metal, jugs of used oil and grease, tattered cardboard boxes, and garbage cans overflowing with fast-food bags, recyclable aluminum cans, and candy wrappers. If there was any evidence there, the police surely had collected it during their visit.

Jake turned to leave when something rustled under a pile of trash next to the garbage cans. A noisy rat? A sheet of cardboard shifted. A big noisy rat? Curious, Jake took a step closer and saw a piece of cloth in a gap between the pieces of debris. Tweed? Someone tossed their jacket in this mess?

As Jake got closer, deep, slow breathing rumbled from below. Was someone sleeping under the pile of garbage? He slowly lifted the large piece of cardboard. The stench of stale urine exploded in his nostrils. Jake took a step back, eyes stinging. He held his breath and inspected the grizzled face of a man snoozing in the pile of discards.

Tammy emerged from the building and yelled at the man, "Hey, you! How many fucking times do I have to tell you to keep the hell out of our yard?" She grabbed a piece of pipe from the heap and rushed the prone figure. Jake leapt aside.

Tammy swung the pipe; the man rolled out of the way; the pipe clanked on the asphalt. "Shit!" She lost her balance and tumbled into the heap of trash. The now wide-wake man scrambled to his feet, ran through the side gate, and disappeared around the building. "Fucker!" she yelled as she got to her hands and knees.

Jake offered his hand to help her up, but she swatted it away.

"Who was that?" Jake asked.

"Some homeless asshole that comes in here at night sometimes to sleep it off. Pisses and pukes all over the place, I think they call him Ballard."

Jake looked around and wondered how she could tell the guy did anything amongst the disaster area.

"Was Ballard here the day Naadir disappeared?"

Tammy sat on the cardboard, scrubbed her chin and said, "Yeah, maybe."

"Do you know where else he might hang out?" Jake asked.

"Who the fuck cares?"

"I do. Any ideas?"

Tammy stood, brushed herself off, and said, "He might spend some time at the homeless shelter on Tully to sleep or the Baptist church on Capitol where they serve meals. That's where the homeless go. They're both close by." She looked down at a fresh grease stain on her jeans. "Shit! I just washed these."

Jake guessed Ballard finished sleeping for the day and would want to get something to eat, so he drove to the Baptist church hoping to catch up with his potential witness in time for lunch. He parked in the lot along the side of the chapel. A stream of men, women, and children filed through a side door of the building. He followed the trail inside.

The multi-purpose hall had folding tables and chairs arranged in long rows across the hardwood floor. People filled the hall eating hot meals served by church and homeless advocate group volunteers.

As Jake walked by the diners, he noted the items served on paper plates: meatloaf with gravy, home-style biscuits, fresh green beans, and milk. Volunteers wearing plastic gloves bused used plates and plastic utensils, cleaned spills, and carried plates for the disabled.

Jake scanned the crowd and shook his head. He only glimpsed Ballard as he jetted from the garage's junk yard. Tweed jacket, torn at the right shoulder. Shaggy dark brown hair. Bulbous nose and bushy eyebrows matching his hair. Tattered blue jeans and running shoes. He would not stand out in the crowd of people in the dining hall.

Jake cruised up and down the rows of tables, peering into the faces of the hungry men.

"Pardon me," a woman's voice said from behind as Jake completed a pass through the third row of tables.

Jake spun and looked down at a woman in her twenties with her blond hair tied in a bun at the top of her head covered with a hairnet. Her gloved hands were full with a tray of emptied plates.

"Can I help you?" she asked. "You don't look like you're here to eat." She glanced at his neatly creased slacks, $300 shoes, and a shirt freshly pressed by the hotel laundry service.

"Yes, I'm looking for a man called Ballard," Jake replied. He gave her the sketchy description of the man he saw earlier that day.

Her brow formed deep furrows. "Who are you?"

Jake looked around at the diners near them, engrossed with their meals. He leaned toward the woman and whispered, "My name is Jake Granger. I'm looking for Mr. Ballard. I think he may have been a witness."

"Witness to what?" She rested the edge of the tray on her hip. The ridges in her forehead grew more pronounced.

"Do you know where Ballard is?" Anxiety grew. He felt time slipping away. "He's not in any trouble. I just need to talk to him."

"Cassandra! Come on. People are waiting here," a man wearing an apron yelled from the far end of the hall. He waved toward the kitchen.

Cassandra yelled back, "Just a second!" She turned toward Jake and glared at him. "You better not make any trouble."

"No. No trouble. I just want to talk to him," Jake assured.

Cassandra's shoulders relaxed, and her forehead smoothed. "I saw Mr. Ballard here earlier." She looked toward the last row of tables. "He likes to sit over there." She pointed and said, "There he is."

Jake looked in the direction she pointed and saw the same back of the tweed jacket and shaggy hair he had seen at Bruce's Garage. "Thanks."

Jake strolled around the table to approach Ballard from the front to minimize the chance of spooking the potential witness. Jake stopped across the table from Ballard, watching him shovel a fork loaded with meatloaf dripping in brown gravy into his mouth.

"Mr. Ballard?"

Ballard jumped from his seat and stared at Jake wide-eyed, cheeks stuffed.

Jake held up his hands as if stopping traffic. "Wait! Don't leave. I'm not here to hurt you. Honest. I just want to ask you some questions."

Ballard chewed and swallowed. "Who the hell are you?" He squinted at Jake. "Wait! You're the guy at the auto body shop." He took a step backward.

"Yes, but I'm not with them. I don't care where you slept. I just wanted to ask you if you saw a man at that garage two weeks ago. Please sit down." Jake motioned to his seat. Jake took the seat across the table.

With Naadir's wife's permission, Jake had snapped a photo with his phone of a framed picture of Naadir. "Do you remember seeing this man?" He placed his phone on the table and slid it toward him.

Ballard sat down and peered into the phone. He nodded. "Yeah. He works at the garage. I've seen him practically every time I go by there."

"Good. Do you remember if you saw him on Monday, March 8, in the early morning? That was two weeks ago."

Ballard stared at him, scratched his head, and grimaced. "Don't assume just because I'm homeless I'm a drunk or a dope addict or mentally ill. I am just unemployed and can't afford to rent an apartment. It's tough on the streets and sometimes I don't remember things as quickly as I used to."

"I didn't mean to imply…" began Jake. "It's just very important to me to find Naadir Please do you recall that day?"

Ballard shook his head, and then his eyes brightened as if a 100-watt bulb switched on inside his head. "I remember now. A bunch of guys in black cars grabbed him and hauled him away." He shook his head again. "They were quick. I wouldn't have noticed if they didn't wake me when he kicked a can over while they dragged him out of the alley."

"Did you tell the cops this?"

"Cops? No, I've never talked to the cops. I heard they were around the shop last week, but I've been hanging out at the church on Capitol. I left yesterday because some guys there were hassling me. I don't need that kind of shit, so I left."

"Did you get a license plate number of the car?" Jake asked in vain.

"No, but they all wore jackets with "ICE" printed on the back."

SEVEN

Thursday, March 25

Constant gridlock ruled downtown San Francisco weekday morning traffic. The maze of one-way streets challenged out-of-town drivers, even with GPS navigation apps. Panel trucks making deliveries to stores and shops obstructed traffic in the middle of the busy streets. Brave or crazy bicyclists weaved in and out of gaps between cars, adding to the chaos. To avoid the headaches, Jake rode CalTrain up the peninsula from San Jose and take two Muni bus transfers to the ACLU offices.

The American Civil Liberates Union of Northern California occupied a building on Drumm Street across from the famed Hyatt Regency-Embarcadero hotel — within walking distance of Justin Herman Plaza and the Ferry Building, popular tourist destinations. Jake's bus stopped on Pine Street, three of blocks from his destination.

Jake walked a few minutes up the slight incline to a modern, four-story building with a limestone facade tucked between a Starbucks and a 7-Eleven. The only way to talk to Naadir in ICE custody was to get a lawyer involved, one that handled knotty immigration issues. Jake had made an appointment to meet with Colin Nguyen, a lawyer with the ACLU. His office was on the fourth floor above the Walgreens pharmacy. The street entrance was an unimpressive pair of glass doors that led to a staircase. Jake climbed to the top floor and entered the office.

The lobby had a simple black marble counter with a receptionist seated behind it. A pair of floor-to-ceiling glass doors to the right of the receptionist led to the lawyers' offices and conference rooms. The office appeared spartan compared to the private law firms Jake had visited in the past. Where the private firms showcased the wealth they had gathered from the exorbitant fees they charged their clients, the ACLU was austere. Colin spotted Jake from his office and pushed through the glass doors to greet him.

"Hello, Jake. I'm glad you came into the City to meet. We've been slammed with preparing cases against the government." Colin shook his hand and led him to his cramped office.

Colin Nguyen was a lanky, thirty-five-year-old with slicked-back, jet-black hair. He had a long, thin face with high cheekbones. He wore a dark blue necktie loose with the top button of his white dress shirt undone. His gray pants matched the jacket hanging on a rack standing next to his desk. He had a fresh shine on his brown Oxfords.

"You were telling me over the phone you believe that Naadir Abdullah is being detained by Immigration and Customs Enforcement," Colin began. He jotted notes on a legal pad as he spoke.

"That's right and he may be a witness or at least a good lead to finding Meghan Harper."

"I've read about her case. You said you are her uncle? I hope they find her soon." Colin shook his head and got down to business. "Abdullah's case is our kind of case, immigration services abusing power. You can't imagine the number of calls we get about this kind of illegal activity by them. Raids in the middle of the night without just cause. Discriminatory sweeps detaining innocents with the undocumented like trawlers snagging dolphins in tuna nets. If we find him, I'd like to take on his case."

"I just want to find out what happened to Meghan."

Colin put down his pen; his chair squeaked as he leaned back. "California is a sanctuary state and Palo Alto, along with many other cities in the state, is a sanctuary city." Jake nodded. "The local police do not cooperate with ICE to enforce federal immigration policies, especially the more punitive or discriminatory ones."

Local sanctuary status put the police at odds with the United States federal government, tasked with enforcing immigration laws and policies. Palo Alto and California refused to cooperate with immigration services to locate and detain undocumented aliens.

"I get that. What's that got to do with Naadir?"

"This deal cuts both ways. In retaliation, ICE won't cooperate with the local cops either — even on a criminal investigation. They won't volunteer any information they might have on criminal suspects they have in their custody. They think there is nothing more important than national defense, and they believe immigration control is at the heart of it." Colin smirked. "I think it makes them feel more important than they really are."

"Does that mean that if ICE has detained Naadir, they wouldn't tell the Palo Alto police?"

"Correct. They will hold him until they fully review his case."

"Given there is bad blood between the PD and ICE. How can I see him, talk to him?"

Colon's lips formed a thin, straight line across his face. He sat up and rubbed his chin, staring at his notepad. He smiled and said, "There is a way," he leaned closer and whispered, "but it's not exactly by-the-book."

Jake whispered back, "I don't care about the book. What do we do?"

Colin called the San Francisco ICE office claiming he was providing Naadir his constitutionally required legal representation. He argued for forty-five minutes with the ICE agent before he won access to Naadir, who was being held in a detention center in the East Bay. He demanded to speak to his client immediately. They agreed to meet that afternoon. Colin cleared his calendar for the rest of the day.

Colin drove Jake to the federal building in Hayward, pressed into service as a temporary detention center when the federal government cracked down on illegal immigrants entering

California. Colin had convinced the ICE agent to allow him to bring an associate with him to meet with their client.

"Remember," Colin said as he parked the car in front of the concrete cinderblock building, "let me do the talking."

Jake made a key locking motion with his fingers in front of his mouth, although he couldn't guarantee he wouldn't butt in when necessary.

They got out of the car and walked into the building through the double doors. They showed their IDs to the guard at the front desk. Agent Hugh MacGregor came out from his office to meet them in the lobby.

"You're lucky you caught up to him now. We're sending him to Texas next week," Agent MacGregor remarked as he led them into the interior office spaces.

"We'll see about that," replied Colin. "The first thing I'll do is request a restraining order."

MacGregor grunted and opened the door to a conference room with a circular table in the center and four chairs encircling it. Jake and Colin squeezed into the two seats facing the door. MacGregor closed the door and sat in the chair next to it.

"Our records show Naadir has the proper visa and has filed paperwork for his green card. Didn't he show you his documentation when you detained him?" Colin asked.

"His name is on a watch list and these guys use fake documents all the time," countered the agent.

"I want to talk to him and I don't want our conversation recorded," demanded Colin.

"Well…" hemmed MacGregor.

"I have the judge on speed-dial." Colin took out his phone and tapped the display. "I'll have a court order within the hour and a call into your boss before you know it." He wagged the phone in front of the agent. "What's it going to be?"

MacGregor sighed. "OK. I'll give you five minutes."

"Fifteen," countered Colin.

MacGregor grumbled as he stood from his seat and left the room.

A few minutes later, he returned with a tired-looking bearded man in an orange jumpsuit and shackles.

The photo on Jake's phone matched the man in front of him. Naadir Abdullah, the Ride-On driver that took Meghan to the Crystal Springs Reservoir.

"Take the handcuffs off him," directed Colin.

MacGregor complied and left the room. Naadir sat in the seat next to the door.

"Mr. Abdullah, I'm Colin Nguyen. I'm a lawyer from the American Civil Liberties Union." He turned toward Jake. "And this is… my associate, Jake. We're here to help you."

Colin spent ten minutes explaining the legal situation to Naadir, who said nothing, but nodded his acknowledgements. Colin outlined his plan to gain his release, then changed the subject.

"Jake would like to ask you a few questions on another matter, if you don't mind," Colin said.

Naadir turned toward Jake with curiosity in his eyes.

"On the night before ICE detained you, did you pick up a Ride-On passenger, a woman named Meghan Harper, from the San Jose Airport and take her to the Crystal Springs Reservoir?" Jake asked. "It was late on a Sunday night."

Nadir furrowed his brow. "Yes, why do you ask?"

Ignoring his question, Jake continued, "What happened to her after you dropped her off?"

Naadir crossed his arms. "What does this have to do with gaining my release?"

Jake glanced at Colin, who shrugged. "I'm her uncle and she's missing."

Naadir's eyes widened. "What?" He covered his mouth with his hand. "She seemed like such a nice young lady. What happened?"

"That's what I'm trying to find out. Apparently, you were the last one to see her."

"I dropped her off at the park-and-ride lot near the reservoir. I asked her if this was OK. It was so late. I've driven people to all kinds of places — some of them questionable, but this place was scary, especially for a young woman alone. I worried about her safety. She assured me everything was fine. She said she was meeting someone. When we got to the park-and-ride, there was a car, lights on, engine running. She got out of my car, spoke to the other driver for a second, waved to me as if to tell me everything was OK, and got in. Everything seemed fine, so I just left. Since I was on the peninsula, I drove to SFO and picked up arriving airline passengers."

"Can you describe the car? License plate?"

"It was a white, four-door sedan. I didn't pay attention to the make or model, and I didn't see the license plate."

White sedan. No license. No other description. Did Meghan know the driver? Jake hated to do it, but he had to talk to Martinez again. The police should stop looking for Naadir and start looking for the driver of the white sedan.

EIGHT

Thursday, March 25

Jake sat in his usual spot in the lobby, waiting. The late afternoon sun blazed through the windows across his feet. He braced for the onslaught, knowing they'd continue their argument from his last visit. Disobeying Martinez's orders exacerbated their strained relationship. A storm brewed in the Palo Alto Police Station.

Anger and frustration creased Martinez's beet-red face as he opened the doors. "Get in here!" Martinez yelled across the lobby.

Martinez marched back to his desk; Jake trailed; neither man uttered a word. The detective sat in his chair and started the argument.

"What the hell do you mean you found him?"

"As I told your receptionist, I found the rideshare driver." Jake smirked. Score 2-0. "He's in ICE custody."

"ICE?" Martinez palmed his forehead. "Shit! He's an illegal?"

"No. There's some mix up, as usual. The ACLU has a lawyer on the case to clear things up." Jake leaned toward Martinez. "He told me Meghan got into a white sedan after he dropped her off. You need to find that car." Jake waited a second for a response. "Did you hear me? Find that white sedan."

Martinez ignored Jake's directive. Instead, he issued a rebuke. "I told you to stay out of police business." Martinez gritted his coffee-stained teeth. He balled his fists on his desk, knuckles white.

"It's just like you to scold me when you should be searching for that car!" Jake's face reddened, frustration grew.

"I'm going to follow procedure. I'm not going anywhere until I talk to Abdullah."

"Does everything have to be 'by the book' with you? I've saved you a step. I'm handing you a solid lead. Can't you at least check it out?"

"I like sticking to 'the book.' I didn't get this far in the department by breaking the rules and 'going cowboy.'" Martinez pointed to his family portrait on his desk. "I have a family to think of. They depend on me and I depend on my career. In this business, you get ahead by painting inside the lines." He picked up his phone. "Now, I have to confer with my superiors to figure out how we can proceed." He dialed a number.

"This is Martinez. I need to talk to you now," Martinez said into the phone. He nodded at the phone and hung up. "Stay here! I mean it." He pointed at Jake. "Don't go anywhere, not even the john." He bolted from his desk and disappeared through a door in the back.

Would the police help or hinder Jake's efforts? More investigators could cover more area. More people searching, conducting witness interviews, searching DMV records. However, police bureaucracy would slow progress. Paperwork, approvals, channels, red tape. Waiting for Martinez to confer with his superiors didn't improve Jake's confidence in the system.

Fifteen minutes later, Martinez reappeared and walked toward a conference room along the far wall with two sour-faced men. Martinez glared at Jake as if reinforcing his previous command to sit.

Jake waited at Martinez's desk while the detective met with his superiors. An hour later, the police chief — Jake recognized her from the online video of the press briefing — marched into the conference room that had swallowed up Martinez; a pair of aides trailed behind her. The expressions on their faces foreshadowed unwelcome news for Martinez. Jake didn't up his mental score against Martinez; he pitied him. But, only for a moment. Martinez deserved what he got for ignoring Jake.

Jake jiggled his leg as he sat on the hard-plastic chair. He watched citizens talk to detectives to deliver witness reports or file complaints. Uniformed officers passed through with suspects in handcuffs.

Jake grinned as he thought about how he had located the missing driver when the police failed. Unfortunately, he hadn't found Meghan. Just another clue: the white sedan.

A man with a familiar face passed along the wall. He spotted Jake and waved. The reporter from Stockton. He rushed to Martinez's desk.

"Jake! What a coincidence meeting you here." Tim McGuire shook Jake's hand like he was pumping water from a well. "Did that search warrant thing work out for you? Is that why you're here?"

"I found who I was looking for." Jake changed the subject. "What are you doing here?" Jake didn't really care why, but talking to the reporter would pass the time.

"I'm interviewing an investigator with the cyber-crime unit. I'm collecting several perspectives for my story. I'm visiting Google tomorrow to speak to their CSO."

Jake nodded. The chief security officer at one of the largest Internet companies surely had plenty of juicy stories to share. However, they probably wouldn't talk about how many times they got hacked every day; that would draw unwelcome attention.

"Can I schedule a time to talk? When are you returning home?"

Jake had promised an interview, but not until he'd found Meghan. He stared at the conference room door, willing it to open so he could learn what Martinez and his bosses planned to do with their newfound information.

As if on cue, the police chief burst from the conference room, red-faced. She shot a glance in Jake's direction and rushed out with her aides trailing close behind. Martinez's bosses left the room next. A moment later, Martinez dragged himself from the room and toward his desk.

Tim spotted the scowling detective trudging toward them. "I'll talk to you later. Call me, please." He side-stepped Martinez, avoiding a collision in the narrow corridor.

Martinez, oblivious to the passing journalist, plopped down in his chair and sneered at Jake.

"You can't imagine the amount of shit you caused me by doing this," Martinez began. "The chief reamed me for allowing you to get involved in this case." He tossed his hands in the air. "This case has suddenly turned from a runaway to a missing person, and you found our prime suspect in ICE custody. The chief has gone head-to-head with ICE before, and each ended in disaster. She didn't appreciate having to deal with them again."

"You're welcome," Jake said with sarcasm and delight at one-upping his former rival. "You would never have found Naadir if I hadn't butted in. ICE would never tell you they had him in custody."

Martinez gritted his teeth. "ICE won't allow us to question Abdullah until after his immigration hearing."

"Thank goodness Colin, the lawyer from the ACLU, has his hearing scheduled for next week." Jake relished the dig at Martinez.

"You think you're so smart. Agent MacGregor found out you aren't an attorney and blames me. He thinks I sent you there, so he's dragging his feet. He's using every piece of bureaucratic red tape there is to make my life miserable."

"Even though there's a criminal loose?"

"Loose? The suspect is in ICE custody. Naadir isn't going anywhere as long as he has an immigration hearing scheduled, but I can't close the case until I get a confession out of him or more evidence." Martinez's eye twitched.

What was that? A twitch? Why? Jake's innate lie detector buzzed. "Naadir is not your man. He told me Meghan got into another car, a white sedan…"

"Right. That's exactly what I'd expect a guilty guy to say. Point the finger at somebody else. Throw us off his trail. That's the oldest trick in the book. Add some doubt into the mix. I wonder; did his lawyer tell him to say that, or did he dream that up all by himself?"

"I believe him," Jake insisted.

"Believing a suspect with a lame story is a luxury I can't afford. I need proof. That's all he said? White sedan, no make or model. No license. No other description. There are probably a hundred thousand white sedans in the bay area. Not good odds of finding the one he says we should look for, especially if this is a phony lead." Martinez flared his nostrils and looked away.

Jake picked up on the unconscious cue. "You're just jealous I found Naadir when you couldn't." Jake enjoyed taking a shot at

Martinez. He hoped it stung after getting reprimanded by his bosses.

The jab hit its mark. "I am not jealous!" Martinez's voice caused others in the room to stop their conversations and turn toward the feuding duo. Martinez looked at the gawkers around him and said, "Get back to work!" Stress mixed with embarrassment creased his face. Tension grew in his shoulders.

"A little touchy?"

"Shut up!" Martinez's voice caught the attention of more spectators.

The outburst startled Jake, prompting questions to pop into his head, queries he overlooked because of his anger with Martinez. Why didn't the police appeal to the public for help to find the driver? Why was his internal lie detector sounding alarms?

"Did you suspect Naadir was in ICE custody all along?" Jake wagged his finger at Martinez. "You didn't want to embarrass the department. Is that why they kept Naadir's name a secret?"

Another eye twitch. "Shut up," Martinez whispered, cautious not to draw any more attention.

"That's it, isn't it?"

Martinez remained silent. What did he and his bosses discuss in the conference room?

Jake continued to press. "Are you going to sit around and wait for Naadir's hearing? What about the white sedan?"

"What about it? Naadir's lying; it's just a ploy. I'm sure of it. I'm not wasting any resources chasing a suspect's desperate attempt to distract us."

"Did you check Meghan's social media accounts? There might be a clue there."

"You computer geeks are all the same. Not everything is about the Internet and social media. Besides, we've checked all of her social media accounts. We've tracked down every lead, and they all came up empty."

"Did you check to see if anyone close to her owns a white sedan?"

"You amateurs! You're grasping at straws. So what if someone she knew owns a white car? I'll bet she has a dozen friends that own white cars. What do you propose? Ask each one of them, 'What did you do with Meghan?'" It was Martinez's turn to fire a salvo of sarcasm. "Besides, why do you assume she knew the person in that sedan?"

"Naadir said she acted like she did. She walked up to the driver, spoke to him, then got in."

"Again, it's part of his ruse. I don't buy it. His story is too convenient."

"So, you're just going to sit around and wait while the actual suspect roams free."

"We will interrogate Abdullah as soon as we can. Then, I'm building a case against him and make sure it sticks."

"I think you should look for the driver of the white sedan."

"And I'm telling you that's a waste of time. We won't go on a wild goose chase."

"You may not have the resources, but I'm…"

"No. You will not investigate this on your own. I'll arrest you for interfering in our investigation." Martinez rose from his seat, planted his palms on his desk, and towered over Jake.

Jake stood and stuck his face into Martinez's. He could smell his cheap aftershave. They sneered and growled at each other like two wildcats. Neither man backed down. Pride and stubbornness wouldn't allow it.

NINE

Thursday, March 25

Social media, the latest playground for the Internet generation. It began as a place to share photos of yourself, the food you ate, your ideas, your pets, your vacations, a place to connect with old friends and make new ones. But it couldn't resist the forces of capitalism. Where there were eyes looking and mice clicking, dollars would follow. The commercialization of social media expanded until advertising dominated what users saw and heard online. Insurance commercials replaced cute cat videos. Offers for premium content flashed and scrolled across screens, drawing attention away from vacation photos and birthday reminders.

Jake again ignored Martinez's order to keep out of the investigation into Meghan's disappearance. He couldn't afford to wait for Naadir to give his statement to Martinez and his cohorts, while the driver of the white sedan roamed free, possibly with Meghan.

Meghan's social media activities could provide clues to the owner of the white sedan. Jake felt it in his gut, but he needed Alexis's help. She knew Meghan better than anyone; she could provide valuable insights as he scoured Meghan's posts.

Meghan knew the driver of the white sedan; she changed her clothes at the airport for him. She talked to the driver; she felt safe getting into his car.

Jake had returned to Alexis's apartment and sat at the dining table. She had prepared dinner — macaroni and cheese. She sat next to him with her laptop open. Their bowls of pasta sat unattended next to them.

"You can see all the pictures and posts Meghan has put up? Right?"

"Sure. We're friends online and in real life. Pretty much everything she posted; I saw." Alexis opened a web browser and went to one of the social media sites Meghan frequented.

"Let's look at the photos she posted. Any pictures or mentions of a white sedan?"

Alexis tipped her head to the side. "That sounds like a long-shot. Meghan isn't a car gal. I can tell you right now; she didn't take many pictures of cars."

"Not the cars themselves, but guys with their cars. Like this one." Jake pointed to a photo taken at the beach with a youthful man and his vintage red Mustang.

"That's Greg and his prized possession. He swore he'd kill anyone that damaged his precious car," Alexis said with a jealous twang in her voice. "If he paid attention to the women he dated half as much as he did that car, he'd get laid every night."

Jake screwed his face. "Too much information. Besides, I don't care about him. His car is red and not a sedan." He pointed to the laptop. "May I?"

Jake flipped through the photos, fingers flying. Selfies, scenery, food, friends. Lots of pictures with guys. "Looks like she dated a lot of guys."

Alexis frowned. "A lot? I wouldn't say a lot. Average, I'd say."

Jake shuddered as he imagined his daughter, Kenzie, dating that many men. It would be impossible to keep up with them, vetting them, making sure they weren't creeps or losers.

Jake examined a set of photos of smiling people holding glasses and eating. "When was this?"

Alexis stared at the photo sequence. "It was last spring. It was a bunch of us getting together at the end of the quarter, after finals, I think." She popped to her feet. "I just thought of something."

"What is it?" Jake looked up at her, puzzled by her abrupt interruption.

"We're looking for someone with a motive."

"And drives a white sedan."

"Yeah, but about three months ago, there was an incident with this guy at a party."

"Tell me."

"I'll tell you, but you can't judge her. It wasn't her fault. It was that guy; he tried to take advantage of her."

Jake waited silently for her to tell the story. She inhaled deeply and blew it out slowly.

"I may have literally saved her ass that night. I'm glad I was there."

On a Monday evening, near the end of the fall quarter, Alexis sat in her bedroom studying for a math test when Meghan burst in.

"Guess who I met today at the bookstore." Meghan panted, bent over, hands on her knees. She wiped sweat from her forehead with the back of her hand.

Alexis didn't bother looking up from her book, knowing there was no way she could guess correctly. "Who?"

"Come on, guess!" Meghan stomped her foot.

"Elvis."

"Be serious. I'll give you a hint. He's on the football team."

Not knowing anyone one on the school's football team, Alexis said, "Ben Roethlisberger," repeating a name she'd heard her Dad mention from his favorite team, the Pittsburgh Steelers.

"Close, he is a quarterback." Meghan squealed. "Nate Spears!"

Alexis didn't follow her college's football team or their players, but the name was familiar from previous conversations with her roommate. Meghan obsessed over him. She claimed he was ruggedly handsome, muscular, and had an alluring grin. Alexis had only seen pictures of him with his helmet on, so she couldn't judge for herself.

"Football player? Really? I didn't think jocks were your type." Alexis teased.

"This one is. You should see him in person." Meghan licked her lips. "We were both in the notebook section of the store, and he started talking to me."

Alexis listened to her friend drone on like an infatuated thirteen-year-old about how alluring Nate smelled up close and how his brown eyes sparkled, waiting for her to get to the punch line.

Meghan finally said, "He invited me to a party at his frat house on Friday night!"

Something didn't seem right to Alexis. Quarterback of the football team invited Meghan, a girl he barely knew, to a frat party. How many other girls did he personally invite? How many would throw themselves at him that night? Alexis knew at least one — the one standing in front of her.

There were several fraternities affiliated with the university. "Which frat?"

"Sigma Tri Xi. You know, the one with the big pillars in front right across from campus."

The fraternity occupied a two-story white Colonial built in the 1920s; it looked like the frat house from the movie *Animal House*, with a similar poor reputation. Censured three years ago for breaking university rules, including hazing and underage drinking, it had clawed its way back to respectability until an incident last year.

"Wasn't a girl raped at a party there?" Alexis reminded her friend, hoping to discourage her.

"Yeah, but they caught the guys. Besides, I'll be with Nate. He'll be sure nothing bad happens."

"OK, but be careful. Those parties can get out of hand pretty quickly."

"You are wound too tight." Meghan's eyes brightened. "I have an idea!"

Alexis frowned. She had seen that look in her eye; it meant something she would regret.

"Why don't you come with me? I'm sure Nate and his frat brothers won't mind. There are so many people at these parties; they won't notice."

Alexis shook her head. "I don't think so."

"If you're so concerned about me, why don't you come along and check it out for yourself?" Meghan's mouth formed a wide grin. "Besides, it will do you good to loosen up; get out and socialize. Who knows, you might get lucky." She winked. "I'm sure Nate has some friends…"

Alexis conceded because she didn't want to have to bail her out of jail at three in the morning. Meghan was right. It had been a tough term. She needed to loosen up, have fun.

That Friday night, the two women arrived at the frat house at ten. People overflowed onto the front lawn. Music blared from huge speakers mounted in the front windows, the heavy beat of the bass thumped their eardrums. Kegs lined the front porch like stout aluminum soldiers. When Alexis walked through the front door, a plume of pot smoke mixed with alcohol assaulted her nostrils, knocking her backward. She stifled the urge to puke.

When Alexis regained her senses, she followed Meghan into the house of wall-to-wall bodies. There were guys and girls paired off, making out in every corner. The roommates pushed their way to the living room where guys competed in a beer guzzling contest. Onlookers encircled them, exhorting them with chants.

Meghan spotted Nate slumped on the couch between a pair of bleached blondes with boobs that strained to stay inside their t-shirts.

"Looks like Nate has his hands full," Alexis said. "Let's get out of here." She tugged on Meghan's arm.

Meghan scowled at Alexis. "We'll see about that. Come on. You're my wingman." Meghan shoved her way through the crowd with Alexis in tow and stopped in front of the star quarterback.

"Hi, Nate!" Meghan yelled over the din. The twin blondes sneered at her.

Nate blinked and looked up at her. It took him a moment to react. "Oh, hi." He struggled to his feet. "I'm glad you could come."

"This is a fantastic party! I'm glad you invited me," Meghan shouted into his ear. She turned toward Alexis. "I hope you don't mind, but I brought my roommate, Alexis."

Nate looked Alexis up and down like she was a used car, then nodded. "Welcome," he said to her.

"Thanks."

Alexis agreed with Meghan's assessment of Nate's appearance. He had the face and body of a Roman god and charisma, a package too good to be true.

Nate led the roommates across the living room toward the kitchen, abandoning his cooing admirers on the couch. They passed a heavy rope hung across the entrance to the staircase leading to the upper floor.

Alexis asked, pointing at the rope, "What's that for?"

"That's off limits tonight," Nate replied, "except for special guests." He winked at Meghan.

The trio entered the kitchen; kegs lined the floor; bottles and cups stood on the counter. "Help yourself." Nate filled a large plastic cup from the keg and handed it to Meghan. "If you're hungry, there are chips and stuff over there." He pointed to the dining area next to the kitchen where a crowd surrounded a table.

Meghan snuggled with Nate at his spot on the couch. The booby blondes left and found other guys to entertain. Alexis nursed a bottle of beer, rebuffing the advances of drunken jocks using slurred pickup lines, and slapping their paws off her butt, until a tall guy with a cleft chin approached.

"Hi, I'm Stallion," he announced through the cacophony surrounding them.

Alexis expected his next line to be, "You wanna ride me?"

"Excuse me?" Alexis leaned away, repulsed by the come-on line.

He leaned in. "I said, I'm Steven," he yelled over the music. His speech was coherent, and his eyes weren't bloodshot like everyone else's.

"Oh. I thought you said something else. I think I lost my hearing a minute after I arrived. I'm Alexis."

"Have you been here long? I just got here. I had a project I needed to finish in the bio lab,"

"Bio lab? Are you studying biology, too?" Steven wasn't like the other guys at the party; he wasn't a jock.

Steven told her he was a senior. His biology project involved applying complex math to analyze the data he'd collected in his experiments, so the math classes he took for his minor came in handy. Alexis needed help with her biology classes, and he offered to study with her. Alexis became so engrossed in conversation with Steven, she didn't notice Meghan and Nate had left their perch on the couch.

When Alexis realized they had vanished, she scanned the room, but couldn't find them amongst the dwindling crowd. Three o'clock. Most of the partiers had left or passed out.

"Excuse me. I have to find my friend," Alexis said to Steven.

Alexis checked everywhere she could on the first floor. They weren't in the kitchen or dining room. They weren't outside, just more passed out party-goers. That left the off-limits upstairs reserved for the "special guests."

Steven caught her looking up the staircase. "Did you find your friend?"

"No. I've looked everywhere. She was with Nate…"

His face fell. "Nate… and his buddies." He tossed the barrier rope aside and climbed the stairs. Alexis followed him to a closed door.

"No. Stop." a familiar but muffled voice protested from inside.

Steven shoved open the door. A shaft of light splashed across two naked men standing next to a bed with another naked man lying on his stomach on top of someone.

Nate turned his head around from his prone position and yelled at Steven, "What the fuck! Get the hell out of here!" He waved his arm.

"Meghan!" Alexis ran to the couple on the bed. "Get off of her!" She pulled on Nate's shoulder. The two onlookers grabbed their pants and ran from the room.

The drunken Nate tumbled to the floor as Alexis pulled the semi-conscious Meghan away. She snatched Meghan's clothes off the floor and yanked her out of the bedroom.

Alexis, with Steven's help, rushed Meghan out of the house and returned home.

Alexis said to Jake, "I haven't mentioned that night to anyone, including Meghan. I doubt she remembers anything."

"Do you think Nate contacted Meghan recently?"

"Nate's the big man on campus. He gets what he wants. I heard he had Steven kicked out of the frat. If he wanted to hook up with Meghan, he'd find a way."

Jake shook his head. "Meghan wouldn't allow that guy to touch her, would she?"

Alexis shrugged. "We need to talk to him. A popular guy like him shouldn't be hard to find."

Jake agreed Nate was a person of interest and worth talking to, but something seemed off.

TEN

Friday, March 26

Jake didn't need to search for a picture of Nate Spears; they plastered his face on the enormous billboard at the entrance to campus advertising the university's sports programs. Carrie Brennan, Stanford's All-American women's soccer forward, appeared next to Nate on the poster, as if they were collegiate royalty welcoming visitors to their realm.

The university's football events webpage announced spring practices had begun that week. The staff planned a media event on the practice field next to the stadium to generate some buzz about the upcoming season. The key players and coaches would be there, an opportunity for Jake to corner the quarterback. Restricted to press members, Jake needed a press pass to enter the event. He fingered the business card in his pocket again.

"I'm glad you called me, Jake," Tim McGuire said. The sounds of several conversations nearby echoed through the phone. "Are you ready to schedule a time to meet?"

"Not yet. I have a condition for this interview."

"Condition? Wasn't getting you the info on that search warrant enough?"

"Thank you for that, but I won't be able to free up any time until I get this job done. I need something from you to do that."

Jake spent fifteen minutes explaining what he wanted and made an irresistible offer to the eager journalist.

"You'll get me an interview with Nigel Brookside, the father of Internet security? In exchange, you want to borrow my press pass for a day?"

"Yes." Jake would have to call in several favors to make it happen, but it was worth it. McGuire agreed. Jake had a ticket to the Stanford football team's media event.

Stanford had finished out of the running for the Pac-12 championship the previous season, but won a bowl game in the post-season. Expectations ran high for the coming year, with Nate as their starting quarterback — having red-shirted his freshman year — and other key players returning for their final year of eligibility.

Jake passed through the gates of the practice field with a hundred other journalists from around the globe, flashing his borrowed press credentials at the cardinal-red-blazer-clad guards.

Following the traditions of the Orangemen of Syracuse and the Crimson Tide of Alabama, Stanford's team mascot was the color cardinal, so they decked everything on the field out in dark red: banners, uniforms, chairs.

The event organizers strategically placed the athletes and coaches in a grid across the artificial turf field. The news hounds assembled around the team representatives to ask questions. The larger crowds assembled around the more prominent players.

Nate, a potential candidate for the Heisman Trophy, drew the largest collection of journalists in the middle of the field. Reporters with audio recorders fired questions, cameramen with their heavy equipment recorded every instant, staff members provided crowd control around the player wearing the number 11 jersey. Getting private time with Nate posed the biggest challenge for Jake.

Jake stood on the outer perimeter of the crowd around Nate. He only caught glimpses of the superstar athlete past the heads of the media hounds. A flurry of scripted questions and rehearsed answers volleyed between the journalists and the star athlete.

"What do you think are your chances of going to the Rose Bowl this year?"

"I like our chances. We have a lot of returning seniors. It takes experience to get into the post-season. And we have talent. I think we have a shot at the national championship." Camera clicks intensified and murmurs rose from the crowd.

"Bold talk for this early in the season; don't you think?"

Gasps escaped from some journalists; others glared at the insolent reporter.

Nate raised his hand to calm his followers. "It takes bold thinking to achieve greatness." Applause and cheers engulfed the scene. These people idolized Nate.

"What about the Heisman for you?"

"I would be honored to be considered, but this season is about our team. Individual awards are secondary." Nate's rehearsed response drew nods from the gathering.

The constant stream of questions and answers continued for an hour until a staff member interrupted the proceedings.

"Thank you all for coming today, but we're out of time."

Other staff members entered the fray and ushered the reporters away from Nate and toward the exit.

Jake saw his opportunity; the team assigned to guard Nate left their positions to move the crowd off the field. Jake rushed toward Nate.

The team's website and program listed Nate as six-foot-one. As Jake approached him, he looked to be closer to five-nine. Too short to be an early round draft pick in the pros. Without pads, he appeared fifteen pounds lighter than the advertised two-hundred-ten. He needed more weight training to survive in the NFL.

"Nate. Where is Meghan Harper?" Jake blurted.

Nate's eyebrows flew up. He leaned away and looked toward his occupied bodyguards. "Who are you?"

"I'm Jake Granger. I'm looking for my niece, Meghan Harper. Have you seen her?"

"Meghan. Harper?" Nate shook his head. "I don't know her." He broke away from Jake and jogged toward the players' exit on the far side of the field.

Jake chased him. "You know her. You tried to rape her three months ago."

Nate stopped. "What the hell are you talking about?" He scanned the field and flagged down a security guard. The guard rushed over.

Jake stepped toward Nate. "Tomorrow's headlines can say you had a great media event, or it can say you attempted to rape a fellow student. Which way do you want it?"

Nate stared into Jake's unblinking eyes. The guard stepped between them, towering over Jake.

"Is this guy bothering you?" The guard held out his hand the size of a catcher's mitt against Jake's chest.

Jake glared at Nate past the guard.

"It's OK. Make sure no one bothers us for a minute." Nate walked around the guard toward Jake.

"What do you want?" Nate shuffled out of earshot of the guard.

"Have you seen Meghan? She's been missing for two weeks."

"Meghan? You mean that girl that disappeared at the airport? I heard about that on the news." Nate shook his head. "I've never met her."

"You don't remember trying to rape her at a frat party? Do you make it a habit of raping girls?"

Nate glanced around. "Can you keep your voice down? I don't need any rumors flying around. I didn't rape anyone."

"I don't care about your reputation. I'd kick your ass right now for assaulting Meghan, but right now, I'm trying to find her."

"Why do you think I know where she is?"

The question stunned Jake. Why? Because Alexis said he might try to attack Meghan again. Was that a good enough reason? Jake needed more validation, another reason to suspect Nate.

"Do you drive a white sedan?"

"White sedan? No. I drive a red BMW 2. It's a two-door coupe, not a sedan. Why?"

"Where were you on the night of March 7, the day she disappeared?"

Nate scratched his head. "What day? March 7?" His eyebrows lifted; his eyes brightened. "I remember that day. I was out of town, and I have lots of witnesses."

ELEVEN

Nate Spears, an outstanding athlete, a guaranteed financial success, and future politician, grew up entitled, and his college career reinforced it. He avoided prosecution because people refused to believe the "golden boy" could do anything wrong. Womanizing and rape. All swept under the carpet, hidden from public view. But he had nothing to do with Meghan's disappearance. His alibi was rock-solid, but something gnawed in the back of Jake's mind, not about Nate.

On March 7, Nate accepted an Academic All-American award in front of five hundred attendees at a gala event in Salt Lake City. There was press coverage, video and photos captured the moment. The festivities continued through the night, followed by interviews and parties. He didn't return to the Bay Area until the afternoon of the 8th. He didn't meet Meghan that night. Another dead-end.

Jake returned to Alexis's apartment to continue his search through Meghan's online artifacts. Jake sat at the dining table in front of Alexis's laptop, flipping through photos. Alexis fidgeted next to him.

"Would you like some coffee?" Alexis stood from her seat and shuffled toward the kitchen.

"Sure." Jake blinked his eyes, weary from staring into the computer screen. He had dashed from his hotel room to meet Alexis and skipped his morning coffee.

A knock at the door. Alexis, halfway to the kitchen, spun and walked toward the entry.

Jake said, "I'll get the coffee while you answer that." He rose from his seat.

"Thanks. There are mugs in the upper cabinet." She opened the front door and gasped. An older man wearing a gray sport coat rushed in, swept her into his arms, and kissed her passionately.

He was in his fifties, gray beard, and crow's feet. He wrapped his arms around Alexis like a boa constrictor, pinning her arms to her sides. There was tongue action in his kiss. He reached one hand down and squeezed her round butt cheek.

Jake peeked from the kitchen and spied them embracing. An image of Kenzie in the arms of an older man flashed in Jake's mind, sending a revolting chill down his spine. Maybe Kenzie could live at home and attend a community college?

Alexis wriggled one hand free and pushed the man's chest, escaping his clutches. "Dr.!"

"I couldn't wait. I had to see you…" The professor's gaze shifted slowly from her face to Jake. He jerked away from her as if he'd stuck his finger in a live light socket, his eyes wide. "I'm sorry. I didn't realize you had company. Perhaps I should have called first."

Jake emerged from the kitchen with two mugs of coffee in his hands. He set the mugs down and faced the professor, eyeing him with disdain.

"Professor Marquis, this is Meghan's uncle, Jake Granger." Alexis motioned toward Jake, stepping toward the shorter man.

Jake extended his hand, and Marquis shook it.

"I just wanted to drop by to check in on Alexis, to see if she needed anything," Marquis sputtered.

Jake glowered at him. "It seems you're the one looking for something."

Alexis stepped between the two men facing Jake. "Professor Marquis was my English instructor last year. He taught both of us, Meghan and me, Shakespeare. He's a wonderful teacher."

"I bet he is," Jake mumbled.

"It's obvious Alexis is in good hands, so I'll leave you two." Marquis spun on his heels and left as quickly as he entered.

Jake peeked through the window and watched the man totter down the stairs with surprising speed to the parking lot. Marquis reached into his coat pocket, pulled out a key fob and pressed a button on it. The lights flashed on a white Lexus parked in front of the building.

"He drives a white sedan!" Jake exclaimed. He bolted out the door, raced down the stairs, and watched the car speed away. "Shit!" Jake slapped his hand on the stair rail and returned to the apartment.

Jake plopped down in his seat at the table. "Professor Marquis looked familiar... You said Meghan was in his class too." He continued scrolling through Meghan's photos. He reached the set of photos he had seen during his last visit, the ones of a party at the end of the term.

Jake stopped on a photo of Meghan standing next to a man resembling the man that had just dashed from the apartment. "Isn't this Professor Marquis?" Alarms went off in Jake's head. The signs of deception became clear.

Alexis leaned in toward the screen and stared. "Yes, so?" She leaned back and crossed her arms.

"He seems awfully cozy with Meghan." Jake studied Alexis's face for the micro-expressions of someone hiding something. How many other female students did Marquis get cozy with?

"I don't know. Maybe he was just trying to fit into the picture.," Alexis fiddled with her phone.

Jake scratched his head. "I don't think so. They're in the center. Look at her smile. She's smiling at him, not the camera. She likes him."

"Sure, she likes him! He's a sweet guy," Alexis blurted.

"A sweet guy that drives a white sedan."

"So what? What are you implying?" She stood and walked toward her living room window, as if intrigued by the fluttering leaves of the sycamore tree outside her building.

Jake turned toward her and said, "He could be the guy Meghan met that night." Suspicion grew in him. "What are you hiding? If you know something, tell me now."

Without taking her eyes off the sycamore, she said, "He was just our professor."

Alexis walked away from the window and wandered into the kitchen. She absent-mindedly opened the refrigerator and peered inside, not looking for anything in particular.

"Was he the driver of the white sedan that night?"

Alexis closed the refrigerator and shouted, "No! Professor Marquis is a sweet man, a genuine gentleman. He wouldn't do anything to hurt Meghan." Her face beet-red.

"I'm not assuming anything, but Meghan got into a white sedan. If that was his car, I need to talk to him, ask him what happened that night."

Alexis's mouth twisted. "There's no way he's involved," she whispered firmly.

Jake nodded. "I understand how you must feel, but I have to talk to him."

Alexis clamped her mouth, silent, upset. She hid something from him, but Jake had more important things to do than reprimand her. He had to find the professor.

TWELVE

Friday, March 26

Stanford's English department in building 460 stood at the top of the Stanford Oval, the loop at the end of Palm Drive at the center of campus. Professor Marquis's ground-floor office was with the other department faculty and staff.

Professor Eugene Marquis had been with the university for twenty years. He received his PhD from Cornell University and came to Stanford after a stint at the University of Kansas, where he met his wife, Julia. They had one daughter, Christine, a junior at Palo Alto High School.

In 1885, Leland and Jane Stanford founded Stanford University, officially named Leland Stanford Junior University, in memory of their son, Leland Jr., who had died of typhoid fever. Stanford's building architecture showcased the university's long, rich heritage. Many of the buildings on campus, including the one that housed the English department, resembled 1800s-era Spanish haciendas, tan buildings with red clay tile roofs; a marked difference from Jake's East Coast university.

Jake taught part-time — until recently — at John Adams University, built in the late 20th century in the heart of Georgetown. Its buildings looked like many of the modern, steel framed and mirrored glassed, commercial high-rises occupying the downtown space surrounding the campus.

Footsteps echoed off the walls as Jake made his way to Marquis's office. He stopped in front of the door with his name.

No lights. He rapped three times on the heavy wooden door. No answer. Jake walked down the corridor into the department office, three doors down.

A middle-aged brunette, hair tied back in a tight bun, sat at a desk near the door, clicking on a keyboard, so engrossed in her work, she didn't notice Jake as he approached. He stood in front of her for a moment, hoping she'd acknowledge his presence when she reached a break in her typing. When she didn't, Jake cleared his throat. The woman jumped.

Her reaction surprised Jake. He thought department administrative assistants would have become accustomed to constant interruptions from students and faculty. Where's the form to submit my grant? Why didn't my expense report get processed? When will they post grades? When's the department meeting?

Recovering from her initial shock, she stared at Jake's unfamiliar face. "May I help you?" she asked in an irritated tone, peering over her computer monitor.

"Sorry to interrupt you," Jake glanced at the nameplate glued to the partition wall, "Suzanne. But I was wondering where I might find Professor Marquis?"

Before Suzanne could respond, a man with salt-and-pepper hair wearing a green sport coat popped through the door and pushed his way past Jake.

"Welcome back, Professor Banks," Suzanne remarked with a broad smile. "When did you return?"

"Last night."

"How was England? You were there four weeks? I bet you got to see all the sights." She handed a stack of folders to the professor. "I got your email. These are the reports you asked for."

Jake stared at the elderly man. He recognized Banks as the chair of the English department from his profile picture on their website.

Banks grabbed the folders and leafed through the top one. "Yes. Yes. My wife insisted on it, even though I was there to teach a seminar." He tottered away, engrossed in the material printed in the folders.

Jake turned toward the assistant. "I'm trying to locate Professor Marquis. He wasn't in his office."

Suzanne looked up at Jake for a second, considering his request. She typed on her computer and said, "Professor Marquis should be in lecture right now."

Jake turned and stared at her. "Can you tell me where?"

She chuffed and checked her monitor. Marquis taught an undergraduate creative writing class at that hour. She gave him the room number and directions.

Jake dashed to the classroom two buildings away to find a hand-scrawled note on the door. Marquis had cancelled the class. Was the professor avoiding him? Had Jake spooked him at Alexis's apartment? Was he on the run? Where did he think he could hide?

Jake raced back to building 460 and again stood in front of Suzanne, still tapping on her keyboard, "The professor wasn't in his classroom. He left a note on the door saying he cancelled the class."

"That's right! I'd forgotten he mentioned he was taking a few days to deal with a personal matter."

"If he's not in his office or in his classroom, where else might he be?"

Suzanne shrugged and returned to her typing.

Jake needed an angle, something to encourage the assistant to cooperate with him. He straightened and pulled his shoulders back, lifted his chin and deepened his voice. "I'm with Bookbinders' Publishing. My company received Professor Marquis's manuscript, and I was in the area. I had hoped to speak to him about it." He gave her a broad, toothpaste-commercial smile.

Suzanne smiled back. "You mean his manuscript about his analysis of the political ramifications of the works of early 19th century American authors?"

Jake wondered why anyone would want to read a book with a subject like that. "Yes. That's the one."

Suzanne clapped her hands once. "That's wonderful. Professor Marquis has been trying to get that one published for years. He will be pleased to hear this."

Jake shuffled his feet and looked down at them. "The problem is… I need to speak to the professor immediately. Another author's project fell through — he didn't meet the deadline. We had hoped to use the professor's book to fill the opening. I'm leaving for New York in the morning and if I don't see him before then, my publisher will find someone else to fill the production gap."

"Oh, my! He was going out of town, but he may still be at home. If you give me your phone number…"

"Thanks, that won't be necessary." Jake sprinted out of the office to his car in the parking garage two blocks away.

Professor Marquis didn't hide his home address. According to the online directory Jake had consulted before he visited the university, Marquis lived a two-minute drive from campus in the faculty and staff housing neighborhood between Stanford Avenue on the southeastern edge of campus and Page Mill Road, a major thoroughfare into the city. Jake cruised down the maple-lined street with one-story homes built in the 1950s. The afternoon sun flicked between the leaves overhead as he checked the house numbers until he spotted a white Lexus in a driveway, the same one that raced away from Alexis's apartment hours earlier.

Jake parked, got out of the car, and approached the professor's house. As he neared the property, the Lexus engine roared to life; the car lurched out of the driveway and raced away. Was Marquis running away? Nothing says guilty more than running. Where did he think he was going? Jake knew where he worked and lived. Did he think he could hide?

Jake spotted another car parked in front, an older car, a classic hand-me-down, dented side panel, worn tires. Someone else was still at home. He rushed to the house and banged on the front door. A girl opened the door, the professor's daughter; she had his sparkling blue eyes. She wore green and white soccer shorts and sucked on a straw connected to a 32-ounce white plastic cup. She stared up at him, waiting for him to speak.

"It looks like I just missed him," Jake announced.

The high schooler loudly slurped the last bits of soda. She nodded with the straw stuck between her lips.

"I'm one of Professor Marquis's students and I have an urgent question for him."

The daughter looked at him suspiciously. "Aren't you a little old for a student?"

"I'm a grad student."

She shrugged and said, "Dad is on his way to the airport. Another one of his business trips. He's going to Japan or China or someplace. I stopped paying attention a long time ago."

"Which airport?"

She scrubbed her head. Her ponytail bobbed. "He's always going away on trips. He was late for his flight out of San Francisco, I think."

Jake weaved through traffic on Highway 101 to San Francisco International Airport. He exited the freeway and drove directly to the short-term parking lot next to the international terminal at the heart of the bustling airport. The professor had a ten-minute head start, but Jake hoped the professor parked in the long-term lot a mile away and had to drag luggage with him, slowing him down. Jake would intercept him before he entered the passenger security screening area.

Jake got off the elevator and ran across the tiled floors. Crowds of passengers gathered around the dozens of different airline check-in counters and automated kiosks. Little chance of locating Marquis in the tangle of bodies; and he may have checked in online, so Jake swam through the crush of passengers toward the security checkpoint, the bottleneck for travelers.

Jake stood breathlessly along the wall to one side of the entrance, examining faces in the crowd, one-by-one. Two minutes, five minutes, ten minutes he waited and observed the flow of passengers. No sign of the professor. Did his daughter give him the wrong destination? Was he in the wrong terminal, wrong airport? Did the professor slip past him in the throng of flyers?

Just as Jake prepared to dash to one of the domestic terminals, he spotted a weary Professor Marquis dragging a disabled roll-aboard suitcase. Jake intercepted him before he entered the line into the security area.

"Professor Marquis," Jake said, blocking his path.

Marquis looked up, crimson-faced and gasping for breath. "Please. I'm late for my flight."

"This is very important and shouldn't take long as long as you cooperate," Jake said in a low, non-nonsense tone.

Marquis squinted hard at Jake. "You were at Alexis's place today. You're Meghan's uncle." He leaned away from Jake.

Jake put his hand on Marquis's shoulder and gripped it, making the older man wince.

"You drive a white sedan."

"Yes, I drive a white car." Marquis shook Jake's hand off and sidestepped around Jake. Jake countered the move.

"Meghan took a rideshare to Crystal Springs Reservoir the night she disappeared. The driver told me she got into a white sedan."

"I don't know what you're talking about." Marquis tried to step around again. Jake took a menacing step toward the shorter English professor.

"The driver also said Meghan seemed familiar with the driver of the white sedan. Was that you? Did you pick her up at that parking lot?" Jake placed his hand on his shoulder again, restraining him.

"I know nothing about that. That wasn't me, and that wasn't my car. Meghan was once one of my students; that's it. If you think I had anything to do with her disappearance, you're mistaken. My flight is about to board. I have to insist you let me pass."

Jake tightened his grip on the professor's shoulder. "Not so fast. I'm not going to just take your word. Where were you on March 7, the night Meghan disappeared?"

Marquis sighed and pulled out his phone. He scrolled through his appointment calendar to March 7 and stared into the screen.

"Our department chair called a faculty meeting that night. It didn't finish until late and then I went straight home." He shook his shoulder free from Jake's grasp.

Jake recalled the conversation he overheard at the English department office. "You're lying. Professor Banks has been out of the country for the past month." Jake's eyes locked onto the professor's willing him to come clean with the truth.

Beads of sweat formed on Marquis's forehead; his jaw clenched. Then, his cheeks drooped like a deflated toy balloon.

"Tell me the truth. Where were you that night?" Jake pointed toward the growing line in front of the security checkpoint. "I wouldn't want you to miss your flight."

Marquis exhaled through gritted teeth. "I was with a woman," he muttered.

"What woman?"

Marquis remained silent.

"Tell me or your wife finds out about your affairs with your female students. Hell, I might even tell Professor Banks," Jake bluffed. He didn't care about revealing the professor's sex habits. He just wanted to find Meghan.

Marquis glared at Jake. "No! You mustn't; it would ruin me."

"OK. Tell me who you were with." Jake stood with his arms folded across his chest. "I'm in no hurry. I have nowhere else to go. We can stand here all day."

"OK. I'll tell you, but no one can find out."

Jake nodded his agreement. "Just tell me the truth."

Marquis whispered his alibi in Jake's ear. He added, "I like Meghan. I hope you find her. If you ask me, you should be checking into her ex-boyfriend. She complained about him constantly. He sounds like a real psycho."

THIRTEEN

Friday, March 26

Jake drove from the airport along Highway 101 through afternoon commute traffic back to Palo Alto, the San Francisco Bay on his left and the peninsula communities, pressed against the Coastal Mountain range, to his right. Warehouses and light industrial buildings mixed with apartments slipped by.

Professor Marquis lied about the faculty meeting, but he had a real alibi for the night Meghan disappeared, something he pleaded to keep secret. Jake didn't care about his secret; he had more pressing issues to address.

Professor Marquis said Meghan's ex-boyfriend had been harassing her, but didn't offer any details. He said Alexis would have more information, so Jake made his way back to her apartment to ask some questions.

When he arrived, Alexis's microwave oven hummed; the aroma of warming curry filled the apartment. The appliance pinged; she opened it, and using an over-sized oven mitt, removed the bowl with the steaming rice dish.

"You want some?" Alexis offered as she carefully placed the bowl on the dining table.

"No. Thanks." The scent of cumin made his stomach growl. "I caught up with Professor Marquis."

Alexis sat at the table and stared at her bowl like she had lost her appetite. "What did he say?" she asked without looking up.

"He had an alibi for the night Meghan disappeared." Jake paused, waiting for a reaction.

Alexis sat unmoving and silent, her breaths shallow; her cheeks glowed pink.

"Meghan didn't get into his car, but you already knew that. Right?"

"I told you. You should have listened to me before you chased after the poor man. I told you he had nothing to do with this." Alexis placed her face in her hands. Her body shook as she sobbed.

"You're his alibi, aren't you?"

Alexis sniffed and wiped her eyes. She took a deep breath and exhaled loudly. "Yes. We were together that night — all night." She looked up at Jake and blinked back tears. "Please don't tell anyone. We didn't do anything wrong. I'm not a student of his anymore." She took another breath. "He's married and I feel bad about that, but his marriage is on the rocks, that's why he asked to be with me."

"You sent me on a wild goose chase; Nick was a diversion so I wouldn't look into Professor Marquis. It was a waste of time. Why didn't you just tell me? Why did you make me hunt him down?"

"I didn't want to betray his trust. I wanted to protect him." Alexis pulled her knees up, hugged them against her chest, and rested her chin on them; she bit her lower lip. She looked like a scolded child.

"You should have trusted me. Now, I don't know what to believe."

Alexis sat upright. "Trust you? What about trusting me? I want Meghan to come home more than anyone. That doesn't mean we have to drag innocent people through the mud and destroy their lives." She crossed her arms across her chest.

Jake shook his head and waved his hands. "I really don't care about Marquis. All I want is to find Meghan."

"So do I!" Alexis pounded her fist on the table. Her spoon bounced and clattered to the floor. "No one wants that more than me."

"OK. Marquis said something about Meghan's ex-boyfriend. What can you tell me about him?"

Alexis screwed her face. "Rick? Rick Reinhardt?"

"Reinhardt? Is that his name? Marquis didn't remember. He said I should talk to you about him. He said this guy's a psycho."

"Psycho? That's a little extreme."

"What did he do? Marquis said Meghan told him this guy harassed her after they broke up."

The corner of Alexis's lip curled. She tipped her head to the right. "Yes, that was true three or four months ago, but nothing since." Her eyes narrowed. She shook her head slowly. "Professor Marquis might be right."

"Right about what? Did Rick have something to do with this?"

"Rick and Meghan, a match made in heaven. Their families had been friends for ages. Rick's dad and Meghan's dad went to college together."

Jake recalled Meghan's father, Charles, attended Northwestern University where he studied business and met Katherine. Charles was a member of a fraternity. Rick's father and Charles may have been frat brothers.

"Rick's a hottie. Tall, fit. Light brown wavy hair that gets in his eyes in the cutest way. Plus, he's a doctor."

"Doctor?" Jake bristled at a long-hidden memory. "He sounds like the kind of guy Katherine would have wanted for Meghan."

"Yeah, that sealed the deal with Meghan's parents. He fit their image of the perfect match for their daughter. He came from a rich family, same social class as them. Good-looking. A doctor. What more could you ask, right?"

"I guess not enough for Meghan."

"No. She didn't like how her parents tried to dictate her life. The more her mother pushed, the harder she pushed back. Plus, he was a jerk."

"What do you mean? What things did he do?"

"Dick stuff. He'd demean her at every opportunity. If she made a mistake — even mispronouncing a word, he'd jump all over her like she'd broken a family heirloom. He never treated her with respect."

"Did he abuse her? Physically?"

"Not physically, emotionally. He'd criticize what she wore or how her hair looked…" She bit her lower lip.

"What is it?" Jake leaned in.

"I heard a rumor he had lost a ton of money gambling and was deep in debt. His parents are loaded, but he had money troubles."

"Do you think his money problems have something to do with this?" Jake recalled his conversation with Martinez. Did he lie about no ransom demands?

"I don't know. It might have stressed him out, sent him over the edge." She shook her head. "If he was my boyfriend, I'd have dumped him a lot sooner than she did. It may sound strange, but Meghan didn't want to disappoint her parents, even though she didn't like them controlling her life. That's the way she was."

Alexis was right. Meghan was an obedient child, wanting to please her mother even if Katherine imposed unreasonable demands on her. "The Argument" came about because Jake saw her behavior headed down a destructive path.

Katherine paced inside the performing arts center front doors. Afternoon heat rose from the concrete porch outside, rivalling Katherine's ire.

Expectant members of the audience, including community leaders, politicians, and music aficionados from across the state, assembled on the lawn, waiting to enter. The piano concert was scheduled to begin in ten minutes. Meghan was the featured performer, a soloist in three pieces in the ninety-minute show, organized by Katherine and sponsored by the city's arts endowment council.

"Where is she?"

"Have you called her?" Jake asked.

She glared at him. "Of course, I have. A dozen times. She's not picking up. It goes straight to voicemail."

"I'm sure she'll get here." Jake glanced at his watch. "She just lost track of time."

"This isn't the first time, but when she shows up, it will be her last." An empty threat. Meghan had proven there was no containing her rebelliousness.

Katherine's phone rang. An unknown caller. "I don't have time for interruptions." She sent the call to voicemail and silenced her phone. Her phone vibrated. "Who the hell is calling me?" She answered the call. "Hello?"

"Mrs. Harper?" an unfamiliar man's voice said. An agitated female voice in the background.

"Yes, this is Katherine Harper. Who is this?"

"Mrs. Harper, I'm Jerry Parker at Aaron's Department Store. I'm the store manager."

"I'm a little busy right now. Can I call you back? My daughter is missing…"

"Your daughter is with us."

Jake accompanied Katherine to the department store. They sat with Meghan, head bowed, in chairs facing Jerry Parker in his office on the second floor of his department store.

"Mrs. Harper, we caught Meghan shoplifting some lingerie…"

"That's impossible! Meghan would never do such a thing," interrupted Katherine. "We give her an allowance. She could buy anything she needs."

The manager held up a handful of lacy thongs. "She tried to take these."

"This is outrageous! What would a twelve-year-old do with those?

"I'm sorry. We have her on video taking them and stuffing them into her purse."

Katherine turned toward Meghan. "What do you have to say for yourself?"

Meghan shrugged without looking up.

"Do you realize how embarrassing this is for me? Not only did you steal, but you disrupted the concert. I have to go back and explain this to everyone." Katherine threw her hands up.

"It's always about you; isn't it?" Meghan mumbled.

"What did you say? Your behavior is disgraceful. I raised you better than this."

"Sis, take it easy. I think what Meghan needs right now is some understanding," Jake interjected. "It was just a mistake. A lapse in judgment."

"Mistake? Like the mistake you and Samantha made? You think you should give me parenting advice? Look at what you're doing to your own daughter!"

Her comment cut into Jake like a knife to his heart. Katherine was right; the divorce had strained his relationship with Kenzie, but he refused to be distracted by her rebuke. "You leave Kenzie out of this. My divorce is between me and Samantha," shot back Jake.

"That's what I'm talking about. You don't realize you've stuck Kenzie in the middle. You can't see how you're affecting her."

Refocusing the argument, Jake said, "We're talking about you and Meghan. Cut her some slack otherwise she'll develop some kind of complex or something."

Katherine bristled and grabbed Jake's arm. "Mr. Parker, please excuse us for a moment." She opened the door and dragged Jake out with her. She shut the door behind them. "Since when did you become a psychiatrist? Meghan is my daughter and I will raise her as I see fit," She hissed.

"That's the problem. You're raising her the same way Mom raised you."

Katherine planted her fists on her hips. "What the hell does that mean?"

"You don't remember how much you complained and wailed about how Mom pushed you, insisted on perfection."

She wagged a finger at him. "I turned out just fine and so will Meghan, if she listens to what I tell her. The world is always watching, especially us. I'm protecting her."

"You're driving her crazy! Someday this will come back and haunt her and you. Her suppressed feelings will bubble up and explode."

"There you go again; talking like Dr. Phil! I object to you sticking your nose where it doesn't belong, giving me your amateur psychoanalysis."

"I love Meghan and I don't want her to get hurt. Pushing her the way you do is not healthy. Please stop."

"No! She is my daughter, and I'm her mother. You have no business telling me what to do."

"I will not stand idly by and let you do this."

Katherine glared at Jake with a laser-like intensity. "You leave me no choice. I forbid you to contact Meghan again. I suggest you leave immediately." She opened the office door. "I have to make this ugly mess go away." She pulled out her checkbook as she re-entered the office.

In spite of his repeated attempts, that was the last time Jake spoke to Katherine and the last time he saw Meghan.

Katherine dictated what was best for Meghan, including whom she should marry. Rick Reinhardt was her choice, not Meghan's.

"What caused Meghan to break up with Rick?" Jake asked Alexis.

"The usual. He cheated on her with a woman he worked with at the hospital. Meghan caught them in bed together one night. He tried to apologize and hounded her for weeks afterward, trying to get her to forgive him. It was pitiful."

"Why would Marquis think Rick had something to do with Meghan's disappearance? Is this guy capable of abducting her? Or harming her?"

Alexis shook her head like she was watching a metronome tapping a rock-and-roll beat. "No, I don't think so. Like I said, I hadn't heard anything about him in months. And when he was bugging Meghan, he was begging her to come back to him like a dog wanting to go for a walk."

"What color car does he drive?" Jake asked.

She combed her fingers through her hair. "Color? I think it's white."

The Yerba Buena Medical Center was a few blocks south of the San Francisco CalTrain station, the end of the line. Rick Reinhardt M.D. was an anesthesiologist at the hospital, a successful one according to Alexis.

Automatic sliding doors swished open as Jake approached the main entrance. The glassed-in lobby extended upward three stories. Jake went straight to the directory mounted to the wall next to the elevators and located Reinhardt's office.

Jake rode the elevators to the sixth floor, stepped out, and looked up and down the long hallway. He followed the arrows on the walls, directing him to room 645. The floor contained doctor's offices, no treatment rooms, so the hall was quiet with only a few people passing through, unlike the overtaxed emergency department on the ground floor.

It was a long shot to find Reinhardt in his office. Doctors were usually in surgery or on the golf course. He could have the doctor paged, but under what pretense? A family emergency? His father was dying? His mother fell ill? His ex-girlfriend is missing?

Jake approached the door marked 645 when a tall man rushed down the hall, pushed past Jake, unlocked the door to Reinhardt's office, and slid inside in one swift, smooth, rehearsed motion. The door shut before Jake reacted. Was that Reinhardt? Jake only glimpsed the man's face. It vaguely matched the profile picture Jake found on the hospital's website.

Jake knocked on the door and tried the handle. Locked.

"Doctor Reinhardt!" Jake banged on the door. "I'd like to speak to you about..." The door opened a crack.

The face of a young man peered around the door. His brow furrowed. "Doctor Reinhardt isn't here. What can I do for you?" He clenched the door.

"I need to talk to him. Can you tell me where he is?" Jake studied the man's face. He had the same hair color as Reinhardt, but he was too young. The skin on his face was smooth. Except for the lack of acne, this man looked like a high school kid.

The kid eyed Jake suspiciously. "Why do you want to talk to him?"

Before Jake could fabricate a story to appease the youth, a man in a dark blue suit tapped Jake on the shoulder. Jake spun to face the interloper.

A gray-bearded gentleman with crow's feet smiled at Jake. He held out his hand and said, "Hello, I'm Doctor Drake. I'm the director of the medical staff here. Are you looking for Doctor Reinhardt?"

Jake shook the elderly man's hand and replied, "Yes, where I can find him?"

The intern came out the door, slipped past Jake and the director with a folder in his hand, and scurried down the hall.

Jake watched the lad until he disappeared around a corner.

The director released Jake's hand, crossed his arms over his chest, and said, "Actually, I was hoping perhaps you might know. He didn't come to work today and we haven't been able to contact him."

FOURTEEN

Jake gazed through his hotel window at the convention center. The CyberSec Conference had ended and with it, went Jake's hopes for landing new clients and generating more income. He would need to find another way to increase Kenzie's college fund. He could go back to teaching; that provided a steady, albeit small, income. His plans would have to wait. Jake was more concerned that he still hadn't located Meghan. All the leads were dead-ends. Jake hoped for more success with his current lead, Rick Reinhardt.

Reinhardt's coincidental disappearance was suspicious. He and Meghan had a history together. Reinhardt obsessed over Meghan and harassed her after their break-up. Not violent, more like a lost puppy in need of nurturing. Meghan knew the driver of the white sedan. Was it Reinhardt?

Did Meghan change her mind? Did they run off with each other? Why wouldn't she tell the people who loved her? Or did Reinhardt trick her to get in his car? Where did he take her?

Jake convinced the director at Yerba Buena Medical Center he could locate Reinhardt, and received permission to speak to the center's IT manager, the person who had Reinhardt's electronic and online account information.

The hospital issued each member of its medical staff a smartphone for business use. The IT department set up the devices with apps and monitored their use. The IT manager gave Jake

Reinhardt's account information, enabling him to use the Locate Phone app to find the GPS coordinates of Reinhardt's phone.

Reinhardt's phone was off. The app didn't receive any signals from it. Jake waited all night for Reinhardt to turn it back on. At 11:00 AM, the app registered a signal; it placed Reinhardt in the city of Pleasanton.

Traffic was heavy with weekend travelers going to East Bay sporting events, picnics, and the mountains. The sun was overhead as Jake crawled along northbound Interstate 880 trapped in the string of cars escaping the urban congestion. The situation was as bad as he'd experienced on the Washington Beltway during workday commutes. Eighteen-wheelers hauling their loads bound for northern destinations competed with autos and buses for space on the roadway. It took Jake an hour to drive the thirty miles to Pleasanton.

Incorporated in 1894, Pleasanton had a population of nearly 83,000 residents and acclaimed as one of the top ten cities in the U.S. to visit by a travel magazine. The city featured year-round community events hosted at its local fairgrounds and stunning outdoor recreational areas. They considered it a bedroom community for San Francisco, Oakland, and San Jose — the metropolitan and commercial hubs of the region, the perfect place to live; that's why Reinhardt's new girlfriend chose it.

Jake had checked the address of the residence where Reinhardt's GPS signal originated; it belonged to Chrissy Chastain, a family physician at the Yerba Buena Medical Center, the co-worker Reinhardt hooked up with while dating Meghan.

Jake followed the directions given by the navigation app into the hills through neighborhoods with manicured lawns and trimmed hedges. He passed a park featuring wide, lush grassy fields and mature oaks; an elementary school, white arrows painted on the circular driveway directed parents for drop-off and pickup; and a fire station with a shiny red truck parked in front.

The navigation app announced the arrival at Jake's destination. He parked and observed the house, assessing the surroundings.

The two-story, wood paneled home stood five miles from Interstate 880 in a tract development. A car covered by fabric stood in the driveway in front of the two-car garage.

Jake got out of his car, crept to the parked car, lifted the sheet, and peeked underneath. A white car, just as Alexis had said, but not a sedan but a Porsche 911. Naadir asserted Meghan got into a four-door sedan, not a two-door sports car. Was he mistaken? Not likely for a guy that spent hours each day around cars of all types. Was this another dad-end? Had he driven there for nothing or was Meghan inside the house — a willing participant or a captive? Only one way to find out.

Jake tiptoed to the front porch and pressed the doorbell. Floorboards creaked from within, approaching the door. A silhouette rushed past the window next to the door.

"Doctor Reinhardt. I'm Jake Granger, Meghan's uncle. I'd like to talk to you." Jake paused and listened for more movement inside. He pounded on the door with both fists. "Doctor Reinhardt! Please, I need to speak to you. I'm trying to locate Meghan," he yelled through the door.

"Did Charlie send you?" a voice replied through the door.

Puzzled by Reinhardt's comment, Jake yelled, "No. I'm not with Charlie. I just want to ask you about Meghan."

"Tell him I'll have the money tomorrow."

"Doctor Reinhardt. I told you I don't know Charlie, and I didn't come for any money."

Reinhard pulled back the curtain; his pale face appeared in the window. He looked at Jake, then looked past him into the street.

"How can I believe you? How do I know you won't bust my head open when I let you in?"

Jake sighed, recalling Alexis's comment about Reinhardt's money troubles. "Let me guess; you owe money to Charlie, a loan shark. You're afraid he's sent muscle out to get it. Am I right?"

Reinhardt squinted at Jake and studied his face. "You said you're Meghan's uncle. You look like her; you've got the same chin, but how do I know this isn't a trick? How can I be sure you're not with the people after me?"

"Think about it. If I was coming after you for money, I'd bust this cheap door down, not knock on it." Jake hoped his reasoning would sink into Reinhardt's skull.

Reinhardt disappeared from view. A moment later the door creaked open two inches.

"What do you want?" Reinhardt asked through the crack.

"I'm looking for Meghan. She's missing." Jake peered past Reinhardt at a neat interior, tastefully decorated, but no sign of Meghan or anyone else.

"She isn't here and I don't know where she is. I have my own problems. Now, go away!" Reinhardt began to shut the door.

Jake shoved his arm through the gap, holding it open.

Reinhardt could have been lying. He could have kidnapped Meghan and held her captive, but his car didn't match the description Naadir gave and there was no sign or anyone else inside.

"You once cared about my niece. She's missing, and I am trying to find her. I need your help. Can I come inside so we can talk?"

Reinhardt paused, then grunted his approval. The door opened wider and Jake slid through; Reinhardt slammed and locked it behind him.

Jake wandered through the front of the house. A formal dining table had a plate with a half-eaten sandwich on it. Jake had interrupted the doctor's lunch. The living room had a fireplace on the far wall with a muted 60-inch TV above it. A leather-upholstered couch faced the TV. Beyond the front rooms was a kitchen and a hallway leading to three open doors — two bedrooms and a bath.

"You don't mind if I look around." It was a statement, not a request. Jake wandered down the hall and peeked in each room — no Meghan.

"I heard Meghan was missing. I'm sorry about that, but I don't know where she is," Reinhardt said. "Wait! How did you find me?" Reinhardt's face flushed. His secret location was out and his safety was in jeopardy.

"I tracked your cell phone."

"Shit! If you could find me, so can Charlie. I have to get out of here." Reinhardt bolted toward the bedroom.

Jake stepped in front of him, planning a palm on his chest. "Not so fast. I need some answers."

"What answers? I told you; I don't know where she is. I have to get out of here before they find me."

"Meghan and I used to be close when she was a kid, but I've had no contact with her since. Who does she associate with? Where might she go?"

"Yeah. She told me about you and how you were her favorite relative, but then you dropped out of her life. She never understood why, and it disturbed her. She thought she had done something wrong."

It wasn't Meghan's fault. The Argument was about her upbringing, but it was between Jake and Katherine.

"When we started dating, our parents went wild. They thought it was wonderful, especially Katherine. To be honest, she was more excited about our getting together than Meghan was."

"What do you mean by that?"

"Katherine gushed about how our match was made in heaven. Meghan always responded with some sarcastic remark like 'Maybe you should date him instead of me.' It was a little weird, but I brushed it off as a mother-daughter thing."

Jake nodded, urging Reinhardt to continue.

"Everything was cool for the first year, but things turned a little weird between us. She had these dramatic mood swings. At first, I assumed it was just some women's hormone thing. One second, she was calm and composed. The next, she's running around hyper, like a chicken with her head cut off, out of control." Reinhardt scratched his chin. "I'm not a psychologist, but she seemed to exhibit some symptoms of bipolar disorder like they described in a psych classes I had in med school."

"Did you talk to Meghan about it?"

"Sure, but she brushed me off. She said I was imagining things, that she was fine."

"But that wasn't what broke up your relationship. Her roommate, Alexis, said you cheated on Meghan," Jake asserted.

Reinhardt gritted his teeth and snorted, "I may have cheated, but I wasn't the only one." His voice trailed off.

"What do you mean? Did Meghan cheat on you?"

Reinhardt shoved Jake aside and ran into the bedroom. "I have to leave," he cried.

Jake followed him into the room. "Tell me," he demanded. He blocked the doorway.

Reinhardt threw a suitcase on the king bed in the center of the room. He pulled out a dresser drawer and dumped its contents into the luggage. He scurried to the closet and yanked a jacket off its hanger and threw it on top of the bed.

"Katherine can tell you. I suspected she knew about it but didn't let on. It was unsettling, and I told Meghan to stop, but she refused. I told her if she didn't stop, I would break up with her. She didn't, so I left."

"What are you talking about? Why should I talk to Katherine?"

Reinhardt zipped shut his suitcase, grabbed the handle, and started toward the door.

Jake held his hand up. "Tell me."

Reinhardt sighed. "Katherine knew Meghan was a sugar baby."

FIFTEEN

Jake gazed out the window from his seat in the back of the plane as the clouds whipped past. Through the breaks below, he spotted vast fields and rural towns. Ahead, the Rocky Mountains and his dreaded destination loomed.

Meghan a sugar baby? One of those young women who dated older men willing to spend money on them for companionship. A mutually beneficial arrangement. That's what the sugar baby/sugar daddy websites advertised. The websites specifically omitted mentioning any sexual relationships — that would be prostitution and illegal in most states. Instead, they promoted themselves as a place to grow relationships; where sugar daddies, usually older, rich men, pampered their sugar babies with money, fine meals, exotic trips, and extravagant gifts. In return, they enjoyed the company of beautiful young women.

Jake shuddered at the image of Meghan in the arms of a fat, old lecher pawing and pressing against her. Why would she subject herself to that?

Jake and Katherine hadn't communicated since their argument over Meghan. No phone calls, no letters, no birthday cards, no texts. They had completely cut ties with one another. Katherine blocked all contact with Meghan. She didn't want him influencing her, turning her against her mother; as if that were possible.

Meghan was the prime example of the perfect, obedient child; and that was the problem. In Jake's opinion, she was getting bad directions from her mother.

Perhaps Martinez was right. Meghan may have realized Katherine was smothering her, and finally broke away, a runaway, gaining freedom from her mother's influence and oppression.

Jake cringed at the thought of confronting his sister after so many years apart. The bitterness had only grown, festered, not subsided.

Katherine was four years older than Jake and their parents' favorite. She did no wrong in the eyes of their parents and he did nothing right — a fact Jake resented, prompting him to join the army as soon as he turned eighteen.

As the snow-capped, blue-gray Rockies passed underneath. Jake asked a flight attendant, "How much longer till we land?"

The flight attendant checked her watch. "We will begin our descent soon. We'll be on the ground in Denver in half-an-hour."

As if on cue, the plane slowed and the queasy, sinking feeling of the downward slope on a roller coaster hit his gut. That was nothing compared to the uneasiness he would experience once he confronted his sister face-to-face.

Jake stopped his rental car in front of a closed, ten-foot wrought-iron gate. A two-story granite-faced building lay fifty yards on the other side of the barrier, encircled by a wall of the same material as the home. The structure looked like a hotel, not a personal residence. Charles and Katherine Harper lived in a mansion with an unobstructed panoramic view of the majestic mountain range to the west.

A surveillance camera mounted on a swivel at the top of the wall watched him. A call box with a red button and a speaker awaited. Jake lowered his window and paused, morning sunlight glinting in his eyes. He wondered if they'd let him in. He pressed the button and waited. He looked up at the camera.

"Jake?" a man's voice squawked through the speaker. "Is that you?"

Jake breathed a sigh of relief. He had delayed the inevitable confrontation with Katherine. "Yes, Charles. It's me." Jake was glad his brother-in-law monitored the gate and screened visitors and not his sister. The speaker buzzed, and the gates crept open. Jake drove through and parked in front of the house. The massive dark oak door opened; Charles stood in the doorway.

"Jake, how are you?" Charles extended his hand to Jake and pulled him inside.

Charles Harper was five years older than Jake, but his gray hair made him appear much older. The wrinkles in his forehead came from worrying about his missing daughter. Meghan had his blue eyes; his showed the strain of the situation.

Jake was envious of Charles's success. Born into a rich and influential family. Smart and savvy with a Northwestern University business degree, he established a real estate development company that expanded rapidly during a building boom in the Denver area.

Charles didn't flaunt his wealth or success in front of Jake. Whenever the conversation turned toward careers, he'd redirect it toward Jake's accomplishments. He admired and appreciated Jake's service to the country. He was genuinely curious and marveled at Jake's computer security exploits.

"It's beyond me how you computer guys can figure out the stuff to make these things work," Charles had once said as he held up his smartphone. "It's a wonder how those hackers can break into our computers, and more amazing is how you can catch them."

Jake admired Charles not only for his business prowess but for his humility.

"I may have a large operation, but I got some lucky breaks. It takes real brains to figure out the stuff you do. I think that's amazing."

Charles was a financial success, but his weakness was Katherine. He would do anything for her. He did anything she asked of him. In the business world, Charles was king. In the universe revolving around Katherine, he was her lowly servant, especially in child-rearing.

Charles provided for Meghan. He gave her whatever Katherine told him she needed. He loved her, but only in the ways Katherine allowed. He knew better than to defy her. Jake never learned that lesson and paid the price.

Charles led Jake into the receiving room off the foyer. He motioned for Jake to sit in one of the two over-stuffed leather easy chairs in front of the fireplace.

"Would you like a drink?" Charles offered, standing next to the wet bar in the corner of the room.

"No, thank you." Jake looked around the dark mahogany-walled room. An antique floor lamp with a stained-glass shade. Leather-bound books on the shelves. The fireplace crackled with glowing, thick, hardwood logs. The leather crunched as Jake fidgeted in his seat.

Charles pulled a plastic water bottle from the refrigerator behind the bar and sat in the twin chair. "It's been a long time," he said, stating the obvious and letting Jake take the lead.

"Yes, it has." Jake furrowed his brow. "You don't seem surprised to see me." More a question than a statement.

"We've been expecting you," Charles replied. He cracked open his bottled water.

"You were expecting me?" Alarms clanged in Jake's head.

Charles ignored the question. "Katherine is around somewhere. I'm sure you'd like to speak to her."

"Yes, that is why I came, but before I do, perhaps I can ask you something." Jake shifted in his seat to face Charles.

Charles nodded but said nothing.

Katherine entered the room. "Charles. Who are you talking to?" She stopped and glared at Jake. "What are you doing here?" she hissed.

Jameson followed Katherine into the room. "Jake. It's been a long time, sir." He stepped past Katherine and extended his hand.

Jake rose from his seat and shook the PR man's hand. A firm grip. "I understand you were out in California," Jake remarked. Jameson was the reason Charles knew to expect him. Eyes and ears everywhere.

"I heard you spoke to Detective Martinez. I was in the area and explained to him we don't know where Meghan is."

"And you wanted to keep things quiet," Jake added. Katherine cleared her throat.

"Yes. There is no need for rumors…" Jameson sensed Katherine's displeasure. He examined her expression. His posture telegraphed recognition. "Please excuse me. I have other pressing assignments to attend to." He spun on his heels and closed the door behind him.

Charles stood and faced Katherine, blocking her view of Jake. "Katherine. He should know the truth." He put his hand on her shoulder.

She shoved his hand off and pushed past him to step toward Jake. "Why are you here?" she repeated. Her stare bored in on him.

"I spoke to Rick Reinhardt. He suspects Meghan suffers from bipolar disorder. Is this true?"

Tight-lipped silence.

"He also said she is a sugar baby. He thought the two were related. He also told me he suspected you knew all along."

"Doctor Reinhardt needs to mind his own business and keep his mouth shut," declared Katherine.

"Please Katherine. For Meghan's sake. Even Jameson..." Charles began. He clamped his mouth shut when Katherine shot him an icy glare.

"I'm only here to help. My only concern is Meghan's safety. I came here hoping we could put aside our differences for a second. For Meghan's sake, please talk to me."

Charles interjected, "Katherine. Can't you see? Jake is here to help. We need the help. We need to get control of this situation." Completing his earlier statement added, "Even Jameson can't find her."

Katherine's angry glare melted into softened sorrow. "OK. What do you want to know?"

"How long had you known she had a problem?" Jake asked.

"Since she was a teenager. Her bipolar disorder manifested itself in risky sexual behaviors. We knew we had a real problem when she was thirteen." Katherine told Jake a story about Meghan's childhood, a secret she held from him, from everyone.

The picture windows on the east side of the Mile High Country Club banquet room sparkled. The lush green of the golf course stretched from the building to the creek. Beyond, homes of the rich and famous dotted the valley.

An army of housekeepers had prepared the room for the gala event. Fresh rose and lily bouquets arranged in large, expensive vases from a bygone era decorated the white-linen-adorned tables. China and silver clinked in the kitchen where a team of chefs and servers prepared the luncheon buffet for the illustrious crowd. Thirteen-year-old Meghan wasn't there to eat; she was there to be seen.

Meghan was part of the decorations, like a china doll on display, to be adored. Meghan wore a stylish red dress made by her mother's favorite designer. Last year, she needed a padded bra to fill out the dress properly; this year no such augmentation was needed. Katherine had fussed over her hair and makeup for over an hour. Her natural assets drew attention. Women admired and envied her. Men, even those that had known her since she was a toddler, desired her. Her wardrobe and makeup enhanced her appeal.

The women's club organized the spring benefit for local charities, the largest fund-raising event of the year. Katherine was at the center of the planning and execution of the gala. People from across the county attended, including some state officials. The event generated awareness for the causes supported by the club including: wildland preservation, pre-school education, and food programs for the disadvantaged. Attendees pledged money for the charities, but came to see and be seen, arriving like Oscar-night Red Carpet denizens. The gala was a tax-deductible excuse to have a party.

Meghan had attended those events since she was four. As time wore on, they became part of her routine: hair, dresses, shoes, accessories, makeup. By the time she was ten, she learned to be polite and charming while listening to older women complain about their children. Husbands yammered about the economy and their wives. She had become a talented actress, smiling and engaging the guests in conversation, winning her praise from the adults.

As a young child, Meghan learned how to behave properly in public. Her mother emphasized the importance of their image and how everything she did was a reflection on them. She taught her not to disappoint them — that was a mortal sin.

Meghan's father seemed to relish those affairs as much as her mother. He stood with other stately looking men, drinking hard liquor and laughing at each other's jokes. Charles put up a front like Meghan did. He once told her it was part of the game — a game she didn't want to play, but made the best of the situation.

"Meghan, we're not like regular people," Charles had said at a dinner hosted by the Chamber of Commerce. "Regular people can be themselves because no one cares if they say or do stupid or uncouth things." He took a swig from his snifter. She wrinkled her nose at the smell of the brandy. "We, however, must maintain a certain level of decorum. People watch us because they want to be us. If we behaved like them, who could they look up to?"

Charles began his career as a real estate agent for one of the national chains, but tired of being jerked around and started his own business. He grew his development company into a thriving business with an impressive downtown office he rarely visited because he was too busy closing client deals. Charles and his company developed much of the downtown area. Buildings bore his name: Hampton Towers, Hampton Square, Hampton Mall. People respected him and clamored for financial advice. People wanted to be like him — rich.

Katherine sat at a table surrounded by other women in designer dresses. Katherine made sure hers looked the best, an off-the-shoulder blue dress with a sash. The women dressed like fashion runway models. The outfits looked fashionable, but better suited for women half their ages and weights.

Katherine was in her element, holding court with the other socialites, sharing stories and gossiping. Meghan would someday fill her shoes, which was why it was important for her to attend those functions. She needed to learn how to look right and behave properly, befitting her social status. It would never do to act like "regular people."

Katherine waved Meghan over. It was her signal to stand next to her and pose. Katherine grabbed her elbow and pulled her close.

"This is my little Meghan," Katherine announced, even though Meghan was half-an-inch taller. She presented her like a trophy, smoothing a wrinkle from her dress and picking off a piece of lint.

Meghan fought the urge to fidget and struck a pose worthy of a beauty pageant winner. She tilted her head slightly and smiled with her lips pursed. She looked pleased to be there, but not ecstatic — just the way she rehearsed it in front of her bathroom mirror a million times.

Katherine's friends around the table cooed.

"She's lovely."

"What a beautiful child."

"You look so mature for your age."

Meghan tipped her chin higher and straightened her back, pushing her chest out. No padded bra; it was all her.

"She looks just like you, Katherine."

Katherine bristled at the last statement from Mrs. Williams. She didn't like being compared to her daughter, or anyone. She was the fairest one of all.

She changed the subject. "Meghan helped with this year's 'Be Ready For School' campaign. Her teachers said she did a wonderful job." She racked up the philanthropy points.

Meghan's friends called her "Little Miss Organized." Katherine liked to take credit for that quality in her. Meghan could put together a plan and execute it. Katherine boasted Meghan had her organization gene, as if something like that existed.

When Meghan's class volunteered to stuff backpacks at the local community center for disadvantaged elementary school students one summer, Meghan assembled a team of volunteers, trained them, collected the supplies, reserved the community center, and set up the assembly line. A flawless event. They delivered two hundred backpacks stuffed with pencils, notepads, crayons, rulers, and scissors for the children. A photo of the group appeared in the city's newspaper.

After a few more comments about Meghan's appearance and questions about her age and which school she attended, Katherine dismissed Meghan.

A group of girls Meghan's age sat at a table reserved for the super-rich kids, including Patricia Hastings, the queen bee of the younger set. Patricia's father owned a chain of restaurants and her mother was the president of the hospital board.

Katherine and Patricia's mom didn't get along, a smoldering competition for the top rung of the social ladder. Their daughters shared a similar rivalry, but Meghan did what her mother had told her — she mingled with the other girls. Practice for when she grew up.

"Hello, Meghan," Patricia said with a dismissive tone. "I like your dress. I think I saw it at the boutique, but my mother said it would make me look fat." She smirked.

"I'm sure your mother said that about a lot of dresses you tried on." Meghan sneered at her rival.

"Do you think you'll join the choir in high school next year?" Patricia asked, preparing to take another dig at Meghan.

Meghan was a superb model, but not a talented singer. Patricia, who had been taking singing lessons since she could talk, was the star of the musical shows.

Katherine compared Meghan to Patricia. Why couldn't Meghan be more talented like Patricia? Why didn't she stick with her singing lessons like Patricia? Being the best was the goal; stay on top. The pressure was constant.

As the party wound down, patrons filed out of the hall, some to after-parties, others home. Meghan spotted a handsome man across the room, about thirty, with dark brown hair and eyes to match.

She strode to the man, drawn to him like a moth to a flame, her eyes locked on him.

"Hi, I'm Meghan Harper," she said, tucking a lock of hair behind her ear. "You're Mr. Hastings' nephew, aren't you?"

"Yes, I'm Cameron Taylor," he said. His eyes widened, and he licked his lips like a hungry tiger. He held her hand and caressed it. His touch was tender, like he was handling fragile porcelain.

"I understand you're in the restaurant business too." She had recalled a conversation with Mrs. Hastings about her sister's son. She said he was movie-star-handsome.

"That's right! I'm impressed and surprised. I didn't think my aunt and uncle would mention me to anyone. I run a place in San Francisco's Union Square."

"That sounds exciting. You must be great at what you do. There are many excellent restaurants in San Francisco," she gushed.

There was chemistry, attraction. The world around them dissolved, leaving them alone together. They didn't notice other guests departing. They chatted about some of their common complaints about being born into rich families. Meghan had plenty of friends who came from rich families, but she'd never shared her feelings with any of them. Cameron had a disarming charm that liberated her to express her deepest hidden feelings.

The pair exchanged stories and shared thoughts. They were enraptured by each other. Time flew by until the hall was empty except for the cleaning crew. A janitor dropped his broom. The bang of the handle on the wooden floor startled Meghan out of her trance.

Meghan looked around. "Shit! My parents left without me, again. They probably went out for drinks with their friends and forgot about me. Now I have to find a ride back home myself."

"Let me take you home," Cameron offered.

"I couldn't. I don't want to impose." The response came out like a reflex. She was being polite.

"It would be no imposition. I'd be happy to take you wherever you want."

Meghan's eyes brightened. "Where are you staying? A hotel?"

Cameron's eyebrows lifted. His pupils widened. He chewed his lower lip then said, "I'm staying at the Denver Manor. Do you know it?"

"Yes, it's a wonderful place. Perhaps you can show me your room?" Meghan winked and cuddled his arm; pressing her breast against it.

"I parked my car just outside." He held her hand and led her out of the hall. He gazed into her eyes. "By the way, how old are you?"

"How old do you want me to be?" Meghan replied with pursed lips.

Jake stared at Katherine; his mouth hung open. His mind spun. The image he had of his precious niece exploded into a million pieces. Her innocence had vanished. "How did you learn of this incident?"

"Guilt gnawed at Cameron over what happened. He came to me and spilled his guts. He claimed Meghan lied about her age. When he learned how old she really was, he felt awful about the incident. But we couldn't let anyone know it happened. We paid him to keep quiet, even though if he told anyone he'd be admitting to committing statutory rape."

"Didn't you seek professional help for her? Therapy?"

"We tried, but Meghan refused, violently. We suspected bipolar disorder, but she was never diagnosed," Charles said.

"Besides, we needed to keep things under wraps," added Katherine.

Protecting their Image and reputation was paramount. Charles was a well-known and influential business leader. Katherine was a community leader. Negative rumors about them or their daughter would blow back on them and make them social pariahs.

"That was only the beginning of a string of embarrassing incidents. We had to keep things quiet. Whenever Meghan got into trouble, we took care of it. We paid people to stay silent and influenced officials to bury reports. We did whatever we had to," added Charles. "I cashed in several favors to maintain our reputation."

"Why didn't you keep her at home? Keep an eye on her?"

"We tried. It seemed the more we tried to control her, the more she misbehaved. When she left home to attend college, we had no choice. We couldn't rein her in; we picked up the pieces and hoped we could continue to keep a lid on all of her antics. Keep out of the gossip columns."

"How did she get involved in sugaring?"

Katherine seethed. Her eyes blazed. "I blame her slutty roommate. That whore got her involved in that sugar baby stuff."

"Alexis?"

SIXTEEN

Sunday, March 28

The atmosphere in the apartment was chilly despite Alexis's warm smile as she handed Jake a mug of steaming coffee. Alexis hopped onto the couch, golden locks flying. She tucked her legs under her and turned toward Jake.

"I hadn't heard from you in a while. I began to worry. Did you find Rick? What did he say?" Alexis asked, face beaming.

"I found him," Jake said through gritted teeth. His frustration grew.

Jake had plenty of time to stew over the sense of betrayal he felt for Alexis during his flight from Denver. The latest dead end was Rick Reinhardt, a man on the run but without Meghan.

"Well? What did he say?" Her eyes wide with anticipation.

"He doesn't have her. He doesn't know where she is." Jake's jaw tightened.

"He could be lying. Are you sure?"

"I'm sure." Jake placed his mug on the coffee table. "He's not lying, but I'm not so sure about you."

Alexis's mouth hung open; her eyes widened. "What the hell does that mean?"

"First, you pointed the finger at Nate Spears. I wasted my time chasing him down only to find out you were covering for Professor Marquis. Now, I learn that Meghan is a sugar baby. You should have told me about her sugaring."

Alexis leapt from her seat and glowered at Jake. "I told you Professor Marquis had nothing to do with this and neither does her sugaring," she declared.

"You don't know that! I need more background. Who did she see? Who did she associate with? I'm just trying to find her and you're holding out on me."

"There is nothing wrong with sugaring. It's just dating. Meghan did nothing wrong. I don't want people saying negative stuff about her. I don't want any victim blaming. I don't want people saying Meghan asked for it." Alexis crossed her arms and clamped her mouth shut.

A moment later, she frowned. "How did you find out about Meghan's sugaring?"

"My sister, Katherine, told me."

"You spoke to Meghan's mom? Meghan told me you hated each other."

"Yeah, we still do, but she told me she blames you for Meghan's involvement in becoming a sugar baby."

Alexis stamped her foot into the hardwood floor; the thud echoed off the walls. "How dare she! She's the one who drove Meghan into the state she's in. She made her what she is! She harangued her to be the perfect daughter; it gave her a complex. When I first met Meghan, I knew the facade she put up hid her genuine character. The problem was the way she coped with it." Alexis walked toward the window and stared out. "She started dating men, older guys that doted on her, paid complete attention to her. They gave her the nurturing she desperately craved and missed getting from her parents, especially her mom."

"So, you didn't encourage Meghan to become a sugar baby?"

Alexis turned back toward Jake. "No. We both knew other women, classmates and friends, making some good money sugaring. It sounded simple, easy, safe. We didn't have to do anything with those men we didn't want to. We set our terms. If we didn't get what we wanted, we walked. It sounded like a great deal. We made our decisions independently, and we agreed it was worth a shot. The extra money helps pay the rent for this place."

"How did you get started?"

Alexis told Jake about her first sugar baby experience.

◆ ◆ ◆

Within minutes after posting her profile with some tantalizing photos on the sugar baby website, Sugarelationship.com, Alexis received a message from Mario through the dating app. He liked what he saw and wanted to connect with her. She checked out his profile to learn more about him.

Mario was a Silicon Valley serial entrepreneur. His profile picture showed him to be handsome enough — not that looks mattered much as long as he paid well for her time. He listed his age as fifty, making him old enough to be her father. It didn't matter to her; the older guys were the richer ones — that was the point. Rich, older guys looking for companionship and willing to pay for it. She sought a financially beneficial relationship. Get paid for spending time with a gentleman who took her to exotic places and spent money on her. That was the deal; that was her business.

Mario suggested they communicate via text messaging. She agreed, and they set up a first date at a local bar.

Alexis stood in front of her closet considering what to wear on her first sugar baby date. She wanted something attractive, but not slutty. The red skirt. Too short. Too flimsy. She didn't want him to think sex was on the menu at the outset; it depended on how their first encounter went. She considered jeans for a more casual look, but the bar where they were to meet was a fancy place in downtown San Jose. She chose a dark blue dress with a mid-thigh hemline.

She put on her makeup and double-checked, making sure everything looked perfect. Her mother's voice echoed in his head, "You never get a second chance to make a first impression." She didn't want to think about her mother at a time like that, but the message fit the occasion.

Their first date was intentionally casual, an opportunity to feel each other out. He wanted to date a sugar baby three or four times a month and would pay her twenty-five hundred dollars.

They sat at the bar with drinks in their hands. She had a margarita; he had a gin and tonic. They made small talk — hobbies, likes and dislikes, work, and school. They got to the topic both of them wanted to discuss — the purpose of their first date. What did they want from the relationship?

"I'll be straight with you. My job keeps me very busy. I'm out of town a lot. When I'm home, I don't have time to date women the usual way. Too much hit-or-miss and sorting through emotional baggage. I'm looking for companionship; someone I can spend some casual time together with over drinks or dinner. No hidden agenda or expectations to 'take things to the next level' because for me, there is no next level. No messy emotions." Mario paused and waited for a response from Alexis.

"I'll be honest with you, too. This is my first time. I guess you might have guessed that from my profile, so I'm new to all this. I wanted some extra cash. Who can't use a few extra bucks?" Alexis smiled, realizing Mario probably didn't have that problem. "I'm happy to spend time with interesting guys with no strings attached. To be brutally honest, I'm looking for a fun time, and I enjoy pampering, but I also like to show off a little too. I enjoy getting dressed up and looking nice for my date. I want the admiration."

"Well, it seems to me we are a perfect match," Mario said as he raised his glass and took a sip.

Alexis and Mario dated for six months until he moved out of the area. He gave her a diamond bracelet as a parting gift.

Alexis loved the excitement. Her job grew to mean more than making some money. By meeting these rich, and sometimes powerful, men, she experienced things she never would with anyone else. Fun and exciting things.

"Did things ever get too 'exciting?'" Jake asked.

"Once. With a guy named Conrad."

Conrad was a fifty-two-year-old self-proclaimed swinger, a thrill-seeker — free fall skydiving, bungee jumping off bridges, and swimming in shark-infested waters. He wanted a sugar baby to share the experiences with.

At first, Alexis found his antics amusing; although it scared her to death being in the ocean with the sharks circling their protective cage. She drew the line when he asked her to join him in taking ecstasy. She didn't need the drug to enjoy herself, but he did. She walked out in the middle of a date when he tried to force her to take the party drug. She posted a critical review on the dating app, and his profile page disappeared from the website soon after. She was glad the creeps and weirdos got weeded out quickly.

"What about Meghan?" Jake asked. "Did she get into any similar situations?"

Alexis sighed. "Meghan took risks I wouldn't have, but that was her. There was no controlling her. I know what her mom and dad had to deal with trying to protect her, but if she put her mind to doing something, she would do it."

"And you never thought to mention this to me?"

Alexis glared at him. "There's nothing wrong with dating and having some fun and excitement. There's nothing wrong with dating older guys. There's nothing wrong with letting them pay you for companionship. Sex was optional; it was consensual between adults." She put her hands on her hips. "Plenty of girls our age do it. It's normal. It's no big deal, and it had nothing to do with Meghan going missing." She wagged her finger at him. "I don't like people putting the blame on the victims."

"What are you talking about?"

"You've heard the rumors. People whispering that maybe Meghan did something wrong, that she was asking for trouble. It's a lie! It's all wrong. I don't want that for Meghan. She's my best friend. I don't want anyone to say those horrible things about her. She's a wonderful person. If she's in trouble, it's not her fault."

Jake held up his hands in surrender. "OK. OK. I understand. I'm not blaming her. I'm just looking for leads." Jake stood and took a step toward Alexis. "Think about it. Were there any guys Meghan worried about, any men that scared her, threatened her? Were there any she mentioned that seemed off?"

Alexis flung her hands in the air. "No!" She turned away.

Jake grabbed her by the shoulders and spun her around. "Please. For Meghan's sake."

Alexis looked at the floor; her arms hung by her sides.

Jake repeated in a calm voice, "Were there any dates Meghan mentioned that she worried about?"

Alexis looked up and sighed, "There was this one guy..."

SEVENTEEN

Sunday, March 28

Alexis never saw the guy Meghan worried about, so she couldn't identify him from a picture. She didn't remember his name off-hand, but might if she heard it again. To find out who he was and how to find him, Jake needed to delve into Meghan's records at the sugar baby website, Sugarelationship.com.

"I know Meghan's username on the dating website. It's sugarblast21, but I don't know her password," said Alexis. "How can we get to see her records without her password?"

"We'll try what we did with her Ride-On account. Call them, posing as Meghan, and ask them to give you the account password," Jake suggested. hoping to have the same success they had with the Ride-On customer support representative.

Alexis eagerly called Sugarelationship, pretending to be a desperate Meghan trying to access her online account. "I always wanted to be an actress," she confessed to Jake as she waited on hold for a rep.

When the customer support rep came on the line, she pleaded with him, giving him a sob story. She'd lost her phone and couldn't remember her password, late for a date, and needed to contact her sugar daddy. The rep said, no. She said it was a matter of life-or-death. He wouldn't budge. She begged and cajoled. No effect.

True to their privacy policy, the company protected client information like a junkyard Doberman. The rep refused to release the information to Alexis. She failed.

They tried their ploy a second time, reaching a different customer support rep. The company trained their employees well; Alexis failed again to get the information.

"I guess I'll never win that Oscar," sighed Alexis. "Maybe if I cried more."

"Those guys are serious about confidentiality," remarked Jake.

"I'm glad for that. I wouldn't want my personal account information leaked. That could cause trouble." She shuddered as if a New England winter gust had blown through her. "It hasn't happened to me, but other women have been stalked by men from the site. The stalkers get women's personal information: where they live and work, who their friends are. They follow the women around. Creepy stuff."

Jake leaned back in his chair and considered his options. He had to resort to more drastic measures. A brute force password guessing attack would lock them out of the account after three failed attempts. Hacking the company's client database would yield the data. But if the company's IT guys were as diligent as the reps on the phone, breaking in would take substantial effort and special tools.

Jake sat alone in his downtown San Jose hotel room, illuminated by the dim bulb in the lamp on the desk. The gentle breeze at his back ruffled the leaves of the four-foot ficus in a blue ceramic pot by the open patio door. He hunched over his laptop, typing.

Despite Alexis's pleas to join him in his search, he left her in her apartment and returned to his hotel where he could use his own laptop and his specialized tools. He also didn't want her involved in a crime.

Jake launched his virtual private network. The VPN would help to obscure his electronic tracks. He downloaded several scripts and software programs — tools of his trade — from his university security lab's server. He started with the sugar baby company's public-facing website. Using the site's URL, he found the server's IP address. His first obstacle was to get through the corporate firewall.

In his experience as a security consultant, many organizations — private and public — did a decent job of protecting their perimeters. Most relied heavily on firewalls to handle traffic flows and access controls. Firewalls were well-equipped to do these jobs, filtering network activity and ensuring only authorized users accessed the protected systems. However, once an intruder breached the firewall, there was minimal resistance to attack. With the help of scripts designed to exploit flaws in the firewall's firmware, Jake penetrated the company's network defenses in an hour.

Jake paused as he considered the thousands of computer security professionals that had roamed the halls of the conference center during the past week. Dozens of those attendees could do what he was doing — breaking into a secured network. At least the owners thought it was secure.

Security-conscious organizations conducted risk analyses — a cost-benefit analysis of their security measures. Budget, time, and manpower constraints dictated how much they could invest. They deployed the defenses they could afford and declared the systems secured. Unfortunately, an experienced, determined hacker could breach those defenses.

With a series of test messages, Jake located the database server. With a few more messages, he discovered the server ran a version of the Linux operating system at a patch level a few months old and vulnerable to attack.

Jake's clients, including federal government agencies responsible for guarding national-security-sensitive information, had difficulty keeping up with weekly operating system security patches. He did a quick search of the known vulnerabilities in the version of Linux running on the database server and found an opening.

Jake used more scripts to probe the server until he exploited the vulnerability, enabling him to gain administrator access. He had control of the machine located somewhere in Washington state.

Jake searched the server and found the schema for the open source database containing the sugar baby information. With administrator access rights, it was straight-forward for him to query the database for Meghan's dating history. The company didn't encrypt the database because encrypting and decrypting the data during use would slow the system and elicit customer complaints. He downloaded the information he wanted onto his laptop. The next step: sift through it to find the sugar daddy Alexis mentioned.

When the download finished, the yellow morning sun peeked between the tall, downtown buildings into his room.

Jake returned to Alexis's apartment armed with Meghan's sugar baby data, including her profile details and messages exchanged using the dating app. Potential sugar daddies initially contacted Meghan through the dating app's messaging feature.

"What are we going to do?" asked Alexis, sitting at her dining table with her laptop open.

"I want you to log into your sugar baby account," Jake replied. "I'll go through Meghan's records and I'll have you look up the guys that contacted her."

Alexis scrunched her face. "Then what?"

"If any of those guys seem like the creepy guy Meghan mentioned, we dig further."

Alexis shrugged.

"What bothered you about this guy?"

"He asked her if she would consider S&M and bondage. He said it was adventurous, exciting. I thought it was kinky and scary."

It was Jake's turn to frown. "Sadomasochism? What did Meghan think of that?"

Alexis shook her head slowly. "She likes risks and excitement…"

Jake's frown deepened; a knot grew in his gut. "But…" he asked hopefully.

"But she didn't go for it; and she told him so."

Jake's heart leapt. "Did he mention this in his first messages to her? Can we find S&M mentioned in these records?" He pointed to his laptop displaying the stolen sugar baby server data.

"I don't know. Maybe."

Jake placed his hands over his keyboard. "I'll go through the messages Meghan received and give you the sugar daddy's username. Let's see if we can find him based on what he's posted. OK?"

Alexis turned to face her computer, nodded, and logged into her Sugarelationship account. Her profile page popped up. Her introductory blurb said, "If you like what you see, contact me and let's see if we can make a mutually beneficial arrangement." A photo of her with her back turned wearing only a thong highlighting her toned and tanned glutes. On her left butt cheek was a small tattoo of a dove. Her blond locks curled along her neck. She winked at the camera over her shoulder.

"Nice tattoo," remarked Jake.

Alexis blushed and quickly turned the screen away from Jake.

Meghan had received hundreds of messages from sugar daddies wanting to connect with her. Some messages were innocent — men offering exorbitant sums of money for her companionship; others tawdry and erotic, as if they were soliciting a prostitute. Jake read the usernames one-by-one, starting with the most recent — the day Meghan disappeared.

Alexis searched the website for the men's profiles. Each listed their name, interests, occupation, income, and photos.

"Most of these names are fake. I've dated many married sugar daddies; they didn't want their wives to find out."

"That's OK. If we find a likely suspect, I have ways to find their actual names," replied Jake with confidence.

Alexis raised her eyebrows but continued to search sugar daddy profiles.

The pair had searched through records for an hour when Jake said, "Try this one. Username, bigdaddy69."

Alexis looked at Jake and said, "Subtle," and typed the name into her search bar. "His profile says he's into exotic and exciting things. And he's seeking arrangements with young, energetic, beautiful women interested in going on adventures with him. He promises the encounters would be eye-opening and mutually satisfying." She read the name of the man. "Kevin Bishop?"

Jake stared at her screen. The close-up profile picture depicted a silver-haired man with crow's feet stretching from intense blue eyes. His broad smile showed brilliant, straight teeth.

A full-body photo showed the shirtless man with enlarged pecs and a trim waist. "Does his name sound familiar? Could this be the guy?"

"The name sounds familiar…" Alexis fixed her gaze on the photo of the half-naked man's body and licked her lips.

"It says here he makes $200,000 a year and willing to share it with a girl seeking adventures," Jake said.

"Kevin Bishop. His name is probably fake. He's probably married." She scanned the profile page. "No Gold Star."

"No Gold Star? What's that mean?"

"The Gold Star designation means the site verified his income and identity. This guy doesn't have it, so there's no telling what his actual name is or how much money he makes."

Jake turned back toward his monitor and scanned the messages from Kevin Bishop to Meghan. "Looks like they exchanged several messages. Here's an interesting exchange." Jake read the message between Kevin and Meghan.

Kevin wrote, *I'm really into getting tied up. It's a real turn-on. You said you were interested in new, exciting things. You might enjoy doing this with me. What do you say?*

Meghan replied, *Sounds interesting. I'm always interested in trying unusual things — for a price.*

A chill ran down Jake's spine. He forced himself to continue to read the private and perverse exchange.

Contact me on blather.

"Blather? What's blather?" Alexis asked.

"Blather is an obscure encrypted messaging app used by people on the Dark Web, people who don't want anyone to read their conversations — drug and arms dealers, mostly."

"Meghan and I usually use our phone's text messaging app to communicate with our sugar daddies. Can you hack blather to see what they said to each other?" Alexis asked.

"I'm afraid not. That app secures messages with strong encryption; the NSA can't penetrate it. Don't ask me how I know that."

Alexis shrugged. "Can you find his real name?"

"Yes, I know of a way."

Jake did an image search on Bishop's portrait using a facial-recognition program he had used many times on government projects hunting down attackers. Jake limited his search to the most popular social media sites to shorten the search time.

After two minutes of scouring the Internet, the program returned with a match on a career networking website. Kevin Bishop's real-life name was Alexander Faulkner, a software engineer at SecurStor, a Sunnyvale-based secure data storage device maker. Jake made note of the company's address. More Internet searches yielded Faulkner's personal information.

"He's single and lives in Santa Clara." Jake entered his home address into this phone. He flipped through photos posted by Faulkner on social media. "There are a lot of pictures of him showing off his physique."

Alexis leaned in. Her eyes widened. "He's got muscles, that's for sure. I can see why Meghan would go for him, but there are no pictures of him with friends. I've dated guys like him, narcistic and friend-less."

Jake wrinkled his nose at her quick, stereotyping assessment of a man she'd never met. He continued his web search. Something caught his eye on a website he hadn't heard of.

"What is this website? URnotalone?" Jake asked.

"It's one of those #MeToo-inspired websites where women in abusive relationships share their stories and get support from other victims. Why?" She leaned in to peer at Jake's monitor.

"Check this out. Here's a post from a woman with the username bambigirl27. She doesn't mention him by name, but she posted his picture."

"Brave woman. Posters usually keep things anonymous. If he found this, she'd be in trouble."

Jake read the post from the abused woman.

"I've been dating this man for three months. I won't mention his name because the one he gave me is fake, but I've attached his photo." The image matched Faulkner's sugar daddy profile picture. "We met through a dating site. At first, it was wonderful. He lavished me with expensive gifts — jewelry, clothes, shoes. We went out to fancy restaurants and on exotic trips. It was fun. I loved the attention he gave me. Then things turned dark. He became more demanding, more controlling, more suspicious, and more violent. I tried to break it off, but he found out where I lived and harassed me. I've moved out of California, but I fear for my life. I'm constantly looking over my shoulder. To help me through this, I've posted this to warn other women. I want to expose this demon to the light.

"Beware. He's a real charmer. He draws you in. The money, gifts, and luxury are addictive. I had tied my fortune to his. I felt like I couldn't defy his wishes, no matter how abusive they were. I couldn't get out of the relationship. I didn't know where to turn."

"This post is two months old," Jake said. "The comments from the readers are supportive. They said she did the right thing by leaving him. Here's an example." Jake read the post aloud.

"These abusive misogynists can't continue to do these horrible things to women with impunity. They should prosecute them and make them suffer."

"Wow! I agree with that poster. Now I'm worried that this guy might have hurt Meghan," said Alexis.

"So am I."

Alexis jumped when someone banged on her apartment door. "Alexis! Are you in there?" a woman yelled. She banged on the door again.

Alexis opened the door, revealing a short, elderly woman wearing a white apron and gray bedroom slippers. Her cheeks pink, and she was out of breath.

"Mrs. Whitaker? What is it? Are you all right? Is Samson OK?" Alexis asked, taking her neighbor's quaking hand.

Mrs. Whitaker, a neighbor two floors below, had visited many times in the past to ask Alexis and Meghan to pet sit her precious long-haired dachshund, Samson. Unlike her previous visits, she looked frightful.

"Yes. Yes, I'm fine." Mrs. Whitaker bent over and inhaled deeply.

"Please come in and sit down," Alexis offered. Jake walked up behind her.

"Did you hear? They found Meghan!"

EIGHTEEN

Monday, March 29

The TV news confirmed what Mrs. Whitaker had reported — they had found Meghan, dead. Hikers discovered her body in a park near the Anderson Reservoir south of San Jose, fifty miles from where she was reportedly dropped off by the Ride-On driver.

"We have an exclusive interview with the couple that discovered the body," the reporter on Alexis's TV announced. A gust of wind swept the reporter's brown hair across her face. She held her microphone close to her mouth as the sound of a helicopter rotor hummed in the distance. A man and woman in their thirties wearing matching red sweatshirts stepped into view next to the reporter. Jake and a trembling Alexis sat on the couch with rapt attention.

"The three of us: Mary, our dog, Rusty, and me, were hiking the trail along the lake when Rusty spotted a squirrel and chased after it. I lost the handle on his leash, and he took off into the brush. We searched for half an hour before we caught up with him. Rusty dug something up at the bottom of the ravine. It looked like clothing. We continued digging, and that's when we found the body," the man named in the caption, Joseph Simpson, said.

"At first, I didn't know what I was looking at, then I realized it was a person's body. It was horrible!" exclaimed the woman identified as Carole Simpson.

"Investigators said the woman appeared to be in her early twenties. Blond. Five-foot-seven. Their initial estimate is that she'd been dead for at least two weeks. This matches the description of Meghan Harper, the Stanford student missing since March 7," announced the female reporter. "Police would not speculate on the cause of death until the coroner has completed the autopsy. The police will be at the scene for several more hours collecting evidence."

An aerial view of the ravine appeared on the TV. Foliage from gigantic oaks partially obscured the view of police forensics team members wearing white overalls bent over, scouring the area for evidence. Yellow crime scene tape stretched between tree trunks, defining their search perimeter.

The video switched back to the reporter. "What was she doing here? How did she get here? Was her death an accident or a homicide? We'll keep you posted with updates as we get them."

Alexis clicked off the TV. She sat in silence staring at the blank screen holding the remote loosely in her hand by her side. Tears welled; her body shook. Soft sobs popped from her mouth. Spit and tears fell to the floor.

"No! That can't be. It isn't Meghan. It's somebody else. They don't know for sure. They shouldn't be saying stuff like that on TV," Alexis cried. "Meghan's still out there. They need to keep looking for her. We need to keep looking for her."

Jake wrapped his arm around her shoulder and bowed his head. She dropped her head on his chest. Tears spilled on his shirt.

He also had hoped they'd find her safe and unharmed. He had pushed aside doubts and the possibility that Meghan was dead. Was there a chance the body they found wasn't Meghan? Jake shook his head. Reality hit him, shattering his hopes.

"I'll go to the police to learn more from Martinez. I'll tell him what we found out about Faulkner," Jake whispered.

Alexis leapt to her feet and yelled, "No! Don't tell them. You can't tell them. They can't find out."

Jake looked up at her and whispered, "This is a homicide now, the cops will thoroughly investigate. They will dig into everyone she met, every website she visited, every phone call she made. They'll make the same connection we made between her and Faulkner. Her sugaring will come out."

"Well, you don't have to make it easy for them. Let them find out on their own."

"What's really going on here? You're not making any sense. You know what I'm saying is true. If I don't tell them, someone else will. Now, it's more important than ever that we find out what happened to Meghan."

Alexis pouted and slumped into the couch cushions. She gnashed her teeth. Strain showed on her face.

"It's about the victim blaming; isn't it?" Jake asked. She flinched. "There's nothing we can do about that. People will gossip, and they'll spread unfounded rumors more when the facts aren't revealed. If we go to the police and tell them about Faulkner, the focus will be on him, rather than Meghan." He waited for an acknowledgement. "You know I'm right."

"They'll say she asked for it; she didn't take precautions. They'll say what she was doing was illegal; they'll call her a prostitute. I don't want people to blame Meghan because they will say all sugar babies are asking for trouble. When something bad happens, they'll say the sugar babies are at fault, including me."

"You? Did something happen to you?" Jake asked.

Alexis's lip quivered. Her nostrils flared. She nodded slowly.

"It was about a year ago. I met this guy through the sugar baby app. We had been on a few dates. One night, we had drinks, then dinner at an upscale restaurant. Afterward, he took me to a motel. He didn't want his wife to find out he was a sugar daddy. We had more drinks there. I woke up the next morning, naked in a dumpster on the other side of town. My memory hazy. It devastated me." Her body trembled, and she cried.

Jake took her hand. "You don't have to tell me this if it's too painful."

"No. I have to." Alexis inhaled deeply and let it out slowly. "I made it back home, but I never told Meghan. I didn't want her worrying about me."

Jake nodded to have her continue. He didn't ask more questions in fear of opening raw wounds. He realized why she insisted Meghan call her from the airport; she didn't want the same thing to happen to her friend.

"I was out of my mind with fear, disgust, anger. I thought about killing the guy. I wanted the world to know what kind of slimeball he was. I wanted to tell his wife and tell her she married a psychopath. I spent a week building the courage to go to the police."

Jake's eyes went wide. He leaned toward her, urging her to go on but afraid of what he might hear.

"They told me there wasn't anything they could do. I had waited too long for a drug test or a rape kit. Because I didn't recall any of the details and there were no witnesses, they said if I brought charges against him, he'd claim any sex was consensual. He'd say I was sexually active because of my sugaring. The police said the DA wouldn't press charges, insufficient evidence."

"That's why you don't trust the cops."

Alexis nodded. "They wouldn't help me."

How could he convince her they should talk to the police despite her experience with them?

"I'm sorry that happened to you. Do you know what happened to that guy?"

"No. After I talked to the cops, I didn't even try to find him. I've tried to forget about it, acted like it never happened — until now." She sat up. "I don't want to believe that something like that might have happened to Meghan. If she really is dead, it makes it real. I don't want to believe she might have done something wrong, made a mistake."

Meghan took risks; she couldn't help herself because of her untreated bipolar condition. Meghan was on track toward disaster long before she became a sugar baby.

"Let me talk to Martinez. I'll find out what's happening with the investigation. They must have confirmed her ID by now. If it is her, I want to tell him what we found. And if Faulkner is involved, the police will make sure he pays. How about it?"

Alexis nodded reluctantly.

A dozen television vans with tall antennae parked along the street in front of the Palo Alto Police Department headquarters. News crews were there to cover the press conference. Jake weaved past gawkers on the sidewalk to get inside.

In a large conference room, the police chief wrapped up her question-and-answer session with the media.

"Has the victim's family made a statement?" a reporter in the third row asked.

The chief in her dress blue uniform, hair pulled back so tight it stretched the wrinkles from her forehead, replied, "I will read the statement issued by the Harper family." She shuffled papers on the small podium and said, "The Harper family is in mourning and wishes everyone would respect the family's privacy."

Privacy, more like secrecy. Katherine's way of handling things. They crafted the brief statement to turn the spotlight away from them. What else could Katherine do to maintain her image?

Jake stood against the back wall amongst the cameramen, adjusting their equipment with their eyes glued to their view finders. Jake made eye contact with Martinez standing next to the chief. He was there to field questions when the chief required more details. Martinez frowned when he recognized the face in the crowd.

They trained Martinez to say things that protected the department and kept the public from panicking. He was a natural. Slick hair, brilliant smile, and a confident stance — attributes people found trustworthy. That didn't impress Jake, and it showed in his expression as he watched Martinez step behind the podium to answer some questions about the current status of the case.

"No. We have not concluded the autopsy," Martinez said in response to a query from the reporter from a New York newspaper.

"How confident are you that the body you found is that of Meghan Harper?" a reporter near Jake asked.

Jake frowned. Surely, that was one of the first things they covered in the press conference.

"As the chief said earlier, we have a positive fingerprint match with Ms. Harper. We are conducting a DNA test to confirm the results, but we are confident that the body we recovered is Ms. Harper."

The rest of the Q&A session included questions designed to get the chief or Martinez to speculate or reveal some detail about the case they didn't want to publicize. Much to the dismay of the media hounds, the spokesmen were adept and tight-lipped; they revealed nothing that might bite them in the ass later.

"Was this a homicide or accident?"

"We'll have to wait for the results of the autopsy."

"Why did she disappear?"

"It's still too early in the investigation to tell."

"Was she drugged? Was she sexually assaulted?"

"We'll have to wait for the results of the autopsy."

The banter went back and forth until the department's public relations man leaned toward the chief's ear and whispered something. The chief raised her hand and said, "Sorry folks, but that's it for now. We'll keep you updated once we learn more."

As if the starting gun to the Olympic 100-meter dash had gone off, the reporters sprinted from the room to submit their stories to their editors. The cameramen around Jake pried their eyes from their cameras and picked up the cords and cases around them.

Jake pushed past the escaping mob to catch Martinez before he left the room. Jake grabbed his arm.

"Jake. As you can see, I'm kinda busy here," Martinez said as he shrugged Jake's hand off him.

"I need to talk to you. Now. I have some information about this case."

Martinez glowered at him, gnawed the inside of his cheek, and said, "OK. Two minutes." He spun and walked out of the conference room with Jake following close behind.

Martinez strode to his desk, plopped down in his chair, and said, "What is it?"

Jake eased into the chair across the desk from Martinez and said, "I've been tracking Meghan's movements…"

Martinez held up his hand as if stopping traffic on the expressway during commute hour. "What did I tell you the last time we met? Didn't I tell you specifically to stay out of police business?"

"Yes, but…"

"No buts. I told you to let us do our job. You're not the only one tracking Meghan's movements. We've had detectives reviewing surveillance video, interviewing witnesses and friends. Our cyber team has been digging into her online activities."

"Were you able to recover her phone?" Jake asked.

"Her phone? No, not yet."

"She did everything on her phone. Internet surfing, text messaging, apps."

"Don't worry. It'll turn up, and we'll examine it thoroughly."

Jake shook his head.

Martinez stood up, signaling the discussion was over. "Thanks for coming by. I have to get back to work."

Jake considered what he should say next. He came to talk to Martinez about what he and Alexis had discovered online, but he had second thoughts. Revealing Meghan's sugar baby dating might tarnish her image, but finding her killer was important. "I have a lead. She was dating a man named Faulkner."

Martinez held up his hand in Jake's face again. "And this guy Faulkner drives a white sedan. Right?"

Jake shoved Martinez's hand out of the way. "I don't know yet, but I think you should investigate him and find out."

"We convinced ICE to let us interview the rideshare driver, Abdullah, ahead of his hearing. He repeated his claim that he dropped Meghan off and saw her get into a white sedan. I don't buy it. It's too convenient. We'll continue digging into Abdullah's past — where he's been, who he's associated with."

Jake stood and glared at Martinez. Talking to the stubborn detective was a waste of time. "You go your way and I'll go mine."

"I'm warning you, Jake. Don't interfere!" Martinez yelled at the back of Jake's head as he stalked away.

NINETEEN

Jake left the police station, infuriated by the detective's remarks. Maybe Alexis was right; they shouldn't rely on the police. He ignored Martinez's advice; he would continue digging to solve the mystery of Meghan's death. Like a festering wound, the notion that Faulkner caused Meghan's death gnawed at Jake's gut. He had proof Faulkner was a menace to women. Did that include Meghan? Jake gave in to his urge to act and drove to the address he'd discovered during his Internet search on Faulkner.

It was late morning when he arrived in front of the condominium complex in Santa Clara about half a mile from Levi Stadium, home of the San Francisco Forty Niners football team. The narrow street was devoid of cars; most residents had driven to work. A ten-foot stone wall surrounded the building with an automated gate controlling access to the residents' parking garage. Jake parked in one of the three open slots in front of the rental office reserved for prospective tenants.

Jake sat in his car and watched the sparse activity in and around the complex. An elderly couple left their building, walking hand-in-hand along the sidewalk. A woman in her twenties, wearing a blue skirt, dashed to the street to catch a municipal bus. A man in a red sweater walked his bulldog.

Faulkner's unit was on the ground floor. A black, wrought-iron gate with an electronic card reader limited access to foot traffic into the inner courtyard. Jake searched for a way around the gate. His solution walked toward him from the other side. He jumped out of his car and strolled toward the gate, slowing to intercept the female resident exiting the enclosure.

The woman twisted the handle; the gate creaked open; and she walked toward the street. Jake rushed to the gate and caught it an inch before it closed. He pulled it open and entered.

The courtyard featured an oval patch of freshly mowed lawn in the center, ringed by thirty-foot palm trees and chest-high, dark green shrubbery. Jake strode along the concrete walkway, counting down the unit numbers until he found unit number 117, Faulkner's condo, on the far side. No sign of activity.

Jake knocked on the front door. No answer. He tried the door handle — locked. Front window curtains drawn tight. He pressed his ear against the chilly glass. Silence. Faulkner may have been at the back of the unit.

Anxious, Jake banged on the door. No response. He waited a moment and banged again, louder. He pressed his ear against the door. Nothing. He banged with both fists.

"He's not home," a woman's voice said from behind him.

Jake spun and saw a stout, elderly woman with curly, silver hair wearing a yellow, floral-print dress, standing by the open doorway to the unit next door. She held a spatula in her hand.

"I'm sorry to have disturbed you," Jake said. He eased away from Faulkner's door.

"Are you a friend of Mr. Faulkner?" She took a step toward Jake.

"No. I wanted to talk to him about a business matter," Jake lied.

"I assume he's at work. I haven't seen him in a few days."

Jake wrinkled his forehead. "Does he do that often? Disappear for days at a time?"

"Occasionally. He once told me he travels a lot for work. He may be away on a business trip now." The woman shrugged.

"Thank you and again, I'm sorry for disturbing you."

The woman returned to her condo and closed her door. Jake dashed to his car. Next stop: Faulkner's office.

Jake drove to an industrial park on the edge of Sunnyvale near the bay. The midday sun reflected off the mirrored glass from the taller structures in the area. Armed with a printed photo from Faulkner's company profile and a pair of binoculars, Jake sat in his car in a parking lot across the street from the SecurStor offices. The company had 100 employees — half in Sunnyvale and half in India. Jake was sure he'd eventually spot Faulkner passing through the employee parking lot.

Jake peered through his binoculars, scanning the faces of people leaving and entering the building for the man matching the photo. He saw dozens of employees passing through: well-dressed men and women, probably in marketing or administration, employees in casual clothing, engineers. But no sign of Faulkner.

Jake had been in his car for thirty minutes when he spotted a white Honda Accord pull into one of the parking spaces near the side employees' entrance. A man wearing jeans and a polo shirt fitting Faulkner's general description stepped out and walked with his back to him. He strode confidently toward the building.

The man weaved between the parked cars, reached the entrance, and opened the metal door. Jake strained to glimpse the man's face. The world around him evaporated as he focused on the image in his binoculars a hundred yards away.

Sharp rapping on his window made Jake drop his binoculars. His heartrate spiked and sweat burst through his forehead and underarms. He turned toward a uniformed man staring at him from the other side of the glass, motioning for him to open his window. Jake complied.

"What are you doing?" the contracted security guard asked, pointing to the binoculars now in Jake's lap.

"Just waiting." Jake shoved the binoculars to the passenger seat.

"Do you work here?" the guard asked as an electronic voice squawked something unintelligible over his radio.

Jake mulled over his options. He could tell the truth and get thrown off the premises immediately or worse. Or he could lie and hope the rent-a-cop would continue his patrol or deal with whatever was happening on the other end of his radio.

"Do you work here?" the guard repeated loudly.

"Yes. I'm waiting for a co-worker to pick something up from the office. Then we'll get out of here."

The patrolman frowned. "Show me your company ID, please." He stuck his hand through the window, palm up into Jake's face, close enough to bite.

"I forgot it inside. That's what my co-worker has gone inside to get." Jake had had enough bantering. "What's your name?" He stared at a patch on the guard's shirt with a name embroidered on it. "Evans. I'm sitting here not bothering anyone and you're hassling me instead of working on that problem your buddy reported over that radio." He pointed to the microphone mounted on the guard's shoulder. "Leave me alone or I'll report you." he growled.

The guard stepped back from the car. "Sorry. I'm only doing my job. Someone reported you. I guess they got suspicious. They told me to check it out. I'm sorry."

Jake grinned. "It's OK, Evans. This company is paranoid about industrial spies. They're afraid someone will steal their trade secrets or something. No problem. My buddy will be out in a minute and we'll be on our way and I won't mention this incident to anyone. I promise."

"OK. Thanks." The guard scurried back toward the building.

Jake slumped in his seat and exhaled loudly. He slammed his palm into his steering wheel. An opportunity to confront Faulkner had slipped through his fingers.

Faulkner might not leave the building for hours; Jake couldn't wait; the security guard might return and hassle him again. He wasn't sure the man he saw through his binoculars was his target. He needed another plan to locate him. He decided on a more direct approach.

He picked up his smartphone, looked up the main number for SecurStor, and called it.

The female operator answered. "Good afternoon, SecurStor. This is Becky. How might I help you?"

"Hello, Becky. My name is Howard Sturgis. I'm from American Financial. I'm trying to get a hold of Alexander Faulkner. He was interested in obtaining a home improvement loan with us," Jake lied. Adding details to the lie made it convincing.

"I'm sorry, Mr. Sturgis, but Mr. Faulkner is working from home today," the receptionist replied.

"He's working from home? Are you sure?" Jake asked.

"Yes, I'm sure. He called this morning and told me himself."

Jake ended the call. Faulkner lied. Jake came up with a new strategy, but it required more help from Alexis. She'd withheld critical information from him. Could he trust her?

Alexis stood in front of Jake in her living room with hands on hips, eyes wide. Her cheeks flashed red. "You want me to do what?"

"I want you to date Faulkner," Jake repeated.

"You have got to be kidding. That guy is dangerous. You read what that woman posted about him, about how he abused her. There is no way I'm getting near that animal," Alexis spat. She paced the floor.

"It will be OK. You can trust me. I'll be with you every step of the way. He wasn't at work or at home. I need to draw him out from wherever he's hiding."

Jake argued with her for twenty minutes. It was their best chance to catch the predator. They would make him pay for his crimes. He couldn't be allowed to roam free and attack more women.

"OK. What's your plan?"

"First, introduce yourself to him through the sugar baby app. Get him interested in you, interested enough to get a date."

"I can introduce myself to him. That's easy enough. One tap on the app and it's done." Alexis rubbed her jaw. "Getting him to respond is tougher. How do I do that? I get a dozen invitations from guys every day. Most of them are creeps and losers. I dump them right off. Of the guys left, one or two might interest me, but once I get to talking to them, I rarely end up dating them. Maybe I'm too picky."

A sly grin formed on Jake's face. "We've seen what Faulkner likes. We know what he's after. We can get inside his head and project an image of you he can't resist." His face brightened. "He liked Meghan. We can make you look like her."

Alexis's face fell. The mention of her dead roommate deflated her.

Jake realized his faux pas and quickly added, "Put on the makeup and clothing he prefers."

Alexis shook her head. Doubt shone from her eyes. "There are like eight sugar babies out there for each sugar daddy. Not good odds."

"We have the inside track on this. We can do this. It's worth a try, right? Think of it as another acting role." He gave her wide, puppy-dog eyes.

The mention of acting melted Alexis's resistance. "OK. I'm in."

Alexis spent the next two hours fixing her hair, putting on makeup, and selecting clothes. She took photos of herself to upload to her sugar baby profile, including intimate photos for her private album. Alexis struck seductive poses in see-through and skimpy outfits, sure to make Faulkner drool.

Alexis updated her description on the profile page to include "seeking unique and exotic adventures," and "willing to try anything for some thrills."

"Try including something straight from his profile," Jake suggested.

Alexis nodded and re-read Kevin Bishop's aka Alexander Faulkner, sugar daddy profile. "Here's something I can use."

She tapped into her profile description, "I want to stretch my limits to find the ultimate pleasure."

"Sounds more like you're advertising for porn, not a date," jake remarked. "He's not only interested in sex. He wants dominance."

"Hey! This was your idea. I'm following your lead and this is what this guy is looking for. The sex will lure him. The dominance will lock him in."

Jake held up his hands in surrender. "All set?"

"Yeah." Alexis paused and put down her phone. "If I get a date with him, what do we do next?"

"What do you mean?"

"I mean, what am I supposed to do with him once I've met him?"

"Nothing. I'll step in and interrogate him. I'll get him to confess that he picked Meghan up after her rideshare."

"He won't tell you that! He'll walk out."

Jake's face flushed. "I guess I didn't think this through." He tapped his chin with his index finger. "Let me think…"

Alexis grunted. "I have an idea. This guy is a slimeball. I don't want to spend any more time with him than I have to, but this may be the only way."

"What's your idea?"

"I'll get him to talk; I'll distract him and get him to confess where he was that night."

"Do you think you can do that?" It was Jake's turn to have doubts.

"This may be our best chance. If I can't get him to open up, you can come in and beat it out of him."

Jake nodded.

Alexis held her phone up and tapped the "Send" button. "Here we go." The phone swished.

"How long does it usually take for guys to respond…" Alexis's phone pinged; messages poured in — ten in five seconds.

"This one is him." Alexis tapped on the reply from bigdaddy69. "He's definitely interested."

"Wow, that was quick. Impressive job!" Jake leaned toward her phone. "What'd he say?"

"He wants to text privately over blather."

"As expected." Jake helped Alexis install the secure messaging app used by the underground and established a connection with Faulkner.

Alexis sent a message to Faulkner. *I'm here.*

I want 2 get 2 know you

Alexis made an offer Faulkner couldn't refuse. *I'll give you access to my private photo album. That will give you a better idea.*

A minute later. *Wow u r gorgeous. I can't wait 2 see u in person.*

Alexis had him hooked. *I can't wait to meet you too. You sound exciting. That's what I'm looking for.*

The hungry predator sent a proposal. *Let's set up a M&G.*

"What's M&G?" Jake asked.

"It stands for meet-and-greet, an initial meet up." Alexis put her phone down as if it had suddenly become hot. She bit her lower lip.

"What's wrong?"

"Now that it's becoming real. I'm not sure I can do it."

Jake took her hand. "We are so close. I promise. I won't let anything happen to you."

Alexis steeled herself and picked up her phone. "OK. We have to decide on some things. First, should we make him pay for this first meeting?"

Jake had a puzzled look. "I've never thought about paying for a date."

"Or we can keep it casual and not insist that he pay. It might make it easier for him to say yes."

"It might also give him the wrong impression, that you're desperate. Make him pay. What else do we have to decide?"

"Where to meet him."

"You're right. We need to set the place. It needs to be someplace where I can keep an eye on you, somewhere you will feel comfortable, safe."

Jake and Alexis discussed several local bars and restaurants. They selected one, and Alexis texted the proposal to Faulkner. A moment later, her phone pinged.

"I have a date. Tonight."

TWENTY

Monday, March 29

Jake sat hunched at the bar, playing nervously with the condensation droplets on the side of his glass of beer. Alexis said the place was safe; she'd been there before. Jake wasn't so sure. While some patrons seemed to be trendy, white-collar workers; others looked rougher. He kept her in his peripheral view as she waited in a booth along the back wall to his right.

They had worked out a scheme to get Faulkner to confess to picking Meghan up from the park-and-ride the night she disappeared. Alexis would flirt with him, make him feel at ease, in control. She had done this with many of her sugar daddies. She said that's what they expected; that's what they craved, a little attention and some dominance. She would pretend to hang on every word Faulkner uttered.

Once he was comfortable talking to her, she'd steer the conversation toward that night without naming Meghan. Jake would listen in on their conversation using a wireless microphone Alexis had planted in her dress, recording evidence.

Alexis sipped her margarita. Jake marveled at how relaxed she appeared. She tossed her hair back like she was waiting for a bus. Anxiety overtook Jake; his heart raced, ready to burst from his chest.

Time ticked by. Thirsty people, after a long day at work, filed in, taking the seats and standing in the open spaces between tables. Jake checked the time. Faulkner was late. Alexis calmly nursed her drink.

A well-dressed man in his thirties approached Alexis. It wasn't Faulkner. Jake listened to their conversation.

"Hi. You alone?" the stranger asked.

"No. I'm expecting my date any minute now," Alexis replied with a coy smile and a flip of her hair, sending the poor guy mixed signals.

Faulkner entered the bar wearing a sport coat over a polo shirt. He scanned the crowded room and spotted Alexis with the younger man hovering near her.

Alexis waved at her date. Faulkner weaved and wedged past revelers standing between him and the young blonde. The intruder spotted Faulkner glowering at him and slunk away.

Faulkner brushed past Jake on his way to the booth, gave Alexis a kiss on her cheek, and sat down across the table from her. Jake blocked out the music and noise around him to listen to the conversation in his earbuds.

"You are more beautiful in person than I imagined," gushed Faulkner.

"Thank you," Alexis replied in a sweet, innocent tone. She leaned in, giving him an unimpeded view of her cleavage.

"Who was that guy you were talking to when I entered?" Faulkner asked. A suspicious frown formed on his face.

"Why? Are you jealous?" Alexis asked, toying with him.

Jake cringed. He was afraid she'd scare him away and they wouldn't get the information they came for.

"Jealous? No," he stammered.

Alexis grinned. "Be honest. We should start this relationship off on the right foot. We should be honest with each other; don't you agree?" Alexis batted her long eyelashes at him. "How about it?"

Faulkner sighed loudly. "Yes, I was jealous. I want you all to myself. There. I've been honest. Your turn. Were you interested in that other guy?"

"Nope. Not In the least. I like more mature men. I'm no babysitter." She reached across the table and stroked his hand. "I'm the one that wants to be babied." She puckered her lips.

Faulkner obliged her and leaned across the table and kissed her. "If babying is what you want, I'm your man."

They exchanged friendly banter for ten minutes while they drank — Faulkner had whiskey and Alexis had another margarita. Alexis stroked his ego, oohing and ahhing at his proclaimed achievements. Some of his claims were embellishments; others were outright lies according to his professional online profile. Alexis was careful not to probe too deeply too quickly.

Faulkner tossed his head back and laughed at one of her comments. He bent forward and slapped his hand on the table, knocking Alexi's glass over, spilling her margarita.

"Oh, sorry. Let me get you a refill." He grabbed the dripping glass and rushed to the bar.

Faulkner stood three feet from Jake as he placed an order with the bartender, "Margarita."

The bartender snatched the used glass and prepared a fresh drink. A moment later, he handed Faulkner a newly filled glass.

Before he left the bar, Faulkner pulled a small vial from his coat and emptied its contents into the drink. He picked up the glass and returned to Alexis.

Recognizing the threat to Alexis, the woman he promised to protect, Jake bolted out of his seat to stop the abuser from drugging her. In his haste, he bumped into a burly drunkard standing nearby, knocking his beer mug from his hand, causing it to fall to the floor.

The brute turned toward Jake and slurred, "Hey, watch where you're going."

"Sorry, man. I'll pay for your drink." Jake tried to push past the bigger man.

The drunkard grabbed Jake's arm and said, "Not so fast. Who's gonna pay for my shoes?"

Jake looked down at the man's feet and saw beer dripping from his dirty, worn work boots. "I'm sure they'll be OK once they dry out. I'll take care of you as soon as I help my friend." He took a step around the bigger man.

Two more brutes appeared from the crowd and joined their friend. The three bulls stood shoulder-to-shoulder like a wall of testosterone-fueled hostility, glaring at Jake.

"We'll take care of you now," the leader said. He raised his fist and swung at Jake's head.

Jake ducked and lunged at the aggressor. He drove his shoulder into the man's gut, forcing an exhale from him. The blow staggered the bigger man, but failed to knock him off his feet. His two partners grabbed Jake by the arms.

The leader recovered from the initial blow and wound up for another punch. Restrained by the pair of accomplices, Jake couldn't dodge the blow, and it landed solidly into Jake's stomach, doubling him over.

"Hey! Stop that or I'm calling the cops," the bartender yelled from behind the bar.

"Come on, let's take this guy outside and teach him a lesson," the leader commanded. His compatriots hauled Jake, toes dragging, toward the front door.

Over his earpiece, Jake heard Faulkner talking to Alexis.

"Here you go. I propose a toast," Faulkner said. "To a mutually satisfying relationship."

Jake glanced back toward Alexis and watched her sip her drink. He tried to call out to her, but no words came out.

Outside, the pair of cronies held Jake up while the leader positioned himself to fire another blow. Before he could, Jake kicked out and connected with the larger man's nose. Blood and a yelp spurted from the bully's face. The brute bent over, holding the bridge of his nose; blood staining the concrete.

"You asshole! I'm gonna kill you!" He landed a jab to the side of Jake's head and an uppercut to his ribs.

Jake's knees crumpled. The twin partners couldn't hold him upright. Jake dodged a kick to the head. The drunken man slipped and fell to the ground, breathing heavily. He staggered to his feet, preparing to launch another punch.

A crowd collected around the combatants. Men jostled for position like ancient Roman spectators in the Coliseum, struggling to get a view of the massacre. They yelled but did nothing to stop the beating.

Before the brute threw his next blow, a police cruiser, with lights flashing, stopped in front of the bar. The attackers ran. The cruiser's front doors flew open and two officers pursued them down the street.

The melee over, a few of the nearby observers hoisted Jake to a sitting position on the cold concrete. His legs failed him; he couldn't stand. Blood oozed from the corner of his mouth. His ribs stung with each shallow breath. Between the individuals crowded around him, he spotted Faulkner leaving the bar, holding

Alexis up and guiding her to the parking lot next door. Jake was helpless to stop him. His mouth opened to call out, instead a fiery blast stabbed his jaw. Only a weak whimper tumbled from his lips.

The bartender emerged from the bar to check on Jake.

"You OK, man?" the bearded man asked. "I called the cops."

Jake's jaw stung when he opened it. He nodded. The bartender hoisted Jake to his feet, led him back into the bar and into a seat near the front window.

The bartender rushed around the bar, filled a plastic bag with ice, and returned. "Here. This should help." He handed Jake the cold pack.

Jake gingerly placed the ice to his jaw. When the numbing effects of the ice enabled him to speak, he asked the bartender, "Did you see what happened with the blonde that was sitting in the back?" Jake pointed to the booth Alexis and Faulkner had occupied.

The bartender looked back in the direction Jake pointed and said, "Yeah. They left soon after the fighting started. She looked kind of out of it. The guy said she had too much to drink, and he was taking her home." He shook his head. "I've seen her here before and I know she can hold her own. She only had two margaritas. Anyway, he led her out. She had a hard time walking."

"Do you know where they were going?"

"No. I didn't bother to ask. I called the cops by then."

A police officer entered the bar and stood in front of Jake. "How are you, sir?"

"I'm fine." Jake groaned as he re-positioned the ice pack on his jaw.

"The paramedics just arrived. They can check you out."

Jake waved his hand. "No. I don't need any medical attention. Sent them away."

The cop nodded and waved to his partner who had entered the bar. The partner spun and exited.

"We caught two of the guys that ran. Witnesses said these men started the altercation. You can press assault charges."

Jake waved his arm again. "No. I don't want to press charges. I'm sorry for making you guys come out here, but let them go. This was just a big misunderstanding. I'd rather forget this whole ugly affair."

The cop nodded and took a step toward the door.

"Wait! Did you see a white sedan leave the area about the time you pulled up?" Jake asked.

The officer scrunched his face. "White sedan?"

Jake nodded.

"No. I don't recall seeing any white sedan."

"OK. Thanks." Jake scoffed at the officer's lack of awareness. Weren't cops trained to observe everything?

The officer left. The red and blue lights stopped flashing through the window, and the police cruiser roared away.

A woman in a blue business suit stepped toward Jake and said, "I overheard you talking to the officer about a white sedan. I think I saw it. A man and woman, right?"

Jake nodded. "Did you see them leave?"

"Yeah. I had just parked my car in the lot and was walking toward the bar when I saw this man dragging a woman to a white Lexus. She looked pretty wasted. I asked him if everything was OK, and he was rather rude. That's why I remember him."

"Did you hear them say anything?"

The woman paused and scratched her head. "She said something like, 'Where are we going?' It was hard to tell; she sounded drunk or something. She slurred."

"What did he say?" Jake asked, hoping for a solid clue to where they had gone.

"It sounded like, 'We're going to Uncle Tom's cabin,' but I can't be sure. That's a book, right?"

Jake's shoulders slumped, deflated. The woman misheard what Faulkner had said and filled it in with something that sounded familiar, an old book title. "Did he say anything else?"

"No. He just put her in the passenger seat and drove away."

"Did you see which direction they went?"

She pointed. "That way, toward the freeway."

The freeway. A route that could have taken them anywhere in the state and beyond. No help there. Alexis could be anywhere with a dangerous predator.

TWENTY-ONE

The microphone Alexis wore had gone dead. Her cell phone was offline. Jake had failed in his promise to protect her. She was helpless in the abuser's hands. He had to find out where Faulkner had taken her — fast. Jake got in his car and raced to Faulkner's condo. It was a long-shot. It was unlikely Faulkner would bring Alexis to his home, but Jake had to check it out.

Under the cover of darkness, he sneaked back into the complex. There was no activity in his unit and no white Lexus in sight. Jake tried the next best thing; he knocked on Faulkner's nosy neighbor's door.

The busybody, wearing a long, wool bathrobe, ready to turn in for the night, answered the door. "It's you again. Did you find Mr. Faulkner?"

"No. I was hoping you might have seen him." Jake peeked inside the older woman's condo. The space near the door had newspapers and magazines stacked to the woman's wide hips. Behind her was a bookcase overflowing with books, decorative vases, and miscellaneous vacation souvenirs. Jake admired the workmanship displayed in the shelf to manage the weight of the objects.

"No. He hasn't been back. I would have seen or heard him if he did. The walls in this complex are paper thin. I pay a fortune in association fees every month. You'd think they'd be able to do something about that." She noticed Jake staring over her shoulder.

She turned to look at the bookshelf. "Did you know that Mr. Faulkner built that?"

"What? The bookshelf?"

"Yes. You wouldn't know it by looking at him, but he's quite a handyman. He built the shelf for me and he helped renovate our recreation room." She pointed into the courtyard at a small structure with glass patio doors. "He put up some soundproofed interior walls so we could have a music room where people could play the piano without disturbing the tenants. Wasn't that kind of him?"

Jake nodded.

"We had been asking the property management to take care of that, but they dragged their feet. It took Mr. Faulkner to volunteer to do the work to get them to OK the project. The property manager should have handled it. I don't know why we pay him."

Jake was wasting time listening to her complain. "You're sure you haven't seen him."

"Absolutely. The stuff that comes through these walls! It'd make your toes curl." She shivered like an ice cube had been dropped down her back. Her face lit up. "Maybe I should ask Mr. Faulkner to soundproof my walls like he did for the music room?"

Jake shrugged his shoulders, thanked the woman, and left the building.

Struck out at Faulkner's condo complex, Jake returned to his hotel room to do more research. His fingers hovered above his closed laptop lid. For a fraction of a second, he considered calling the police, but the thought of confronting Martinez made him shudder. He'd accuse Jake of obstruction and ignore his pleas to help find Alexis. He might arrest him for disobeying his orders, again, to stay out of police business.

Jake gritted his teeth and opened his laptop. He stared at the information he'd gathered on Faulkner. Single, never married. Five-foot-eight, two-hundred pounds. Light brown hair. Blue eyes. Software engineer at SecurStor. Before that, he worked at several Internet start-ups in the Bay Area. Three jobs in five years. Condo owner.

The only clue he had was the mysterious and possibly misheard one from the woman who saw Faulkner take Alexis from the bar — the reference to Uncle Tom's cabin. What were the chances Faulkner had an uncle named Tom?

Jake consulted a family heritage website and searched for male relatives of Faulkner. No one named Tom, Thomas, or Tomas. It was possible the woman misheard what Faulkner said. Or "uncle" was an honorific title for a close family friend? Possible, but impossible to trace without more personal information on Faulkner. Did the place remind Faulkner of the cabin in Harriet Beecher Stowe's 1852 novel?

Jake searched online for an hour and found no connection between Faulkner and anyone named Tom. The Uncle Tom lead was a dead-end.

Jake scanned photos on Faulkner's social media. Faulkner had posted dozens of public pictures, some of him with women in a wooded setting — redwoods, pines in the background. They had captions saying, "Having some sugar at my cabin" and "In the woods with my sweet baby."

Did Faulkner own any other property? Jake checked the county public records database. Nothing. He checked the records from the other counties within commuting distance of his jobs over the past four years. Again, nothing. If Faulkner had vacation property in the Sierras or out of state, it would take hours to locate it. Where did he take Alexis?

Jake checked the photos' GPS location metadata embedded by mobile device cameras. To protect user privacy, the popular social media sites stripped off metadata from uploaded photos. The websites Faulkner frequented followed that practice.

Jake searched for clues in the pictures — a landmark, a unique species of tree, or an identifiable rock formation. Jake examined the backgrounds in the photos and found nothing useful. The social media sites were more dead-ends.

Jake broadened his Internet search and found a blog site Faulkner had abandoned; his last post was six months old. An amateur designed the blog site, probably Faulkner himself — simple fonts, few graphics, and an uninspired layout. There was minimal content. The posts included photos and pages of rambling text covering inane topics such as: his pet peeves (slow drivers in the fast lane of the freeway and ugly dogs) and graphic descriptions of his sexual exploits. In one blog post, he bragged about the women he'd taken to the woods. He included a photo of a rustic-looking cabin nestled among tall redwoods similar to some tress in his social media pictures.

Jake checked the metadata of the image. The homemade website failed to remove the GPS location of the photo. The latitude, longitude, and altitude in the metadata showed Faulkner took the photo in the Santa Cruz Mountains, a twenty-five-mile drive from San Jose.

Jake did another public records property search; this time using the cabin's location and discovered it belonged to James T. Herzog, Faulkner's uncle. His middle name was Thomas, a detail the heritage website failed to record.

Jake consulted a satellite map, pinpointed the location, and zoomed in on the grainy image taken from 22,000 miles overhead. The surrounding redwoods partially obscured the roof of a small dwelling. Jake had a lead. He entered the location into his phone's GPS locator app and ran out the door.

The night was pitch black as he sped southbound toward the coast along the winding Highway 17. During commute time, the trip into the Santa Cruz Mountains would take an hour. At midnight, the trip would take half the time, if he didn't get lost on the back roads in the forest.

Highway 17 was the major traffic artery connecting Silicon Valley with the Monterey Bay, the playground of the rugged California coastline, including the Santa Cruz beaches, famous for its surfing. The Monterey Bay Aquarium, Pebble Beach golf course, Santa Cruz boardwalk, and Carmel-by-the-Sea were other world-renown tourist spots in the Monterey Bay region. Motorists blazed through the winding mountain pass at excessive speeds, making Highway 17 a treacherous roadway.

Denizens of Silicon Valley, notorious risk-takers, drove the way they ran their companies — breaking the rules. Rolling through stop signs and making illegal turns was all part of cutting corners to get ahead. To get to the front of the pack, they pressed the accelerator to the floor, figuratively and literally. On the road, the laws of physics took control, and accidents happened.

Highway 17 proved even Silicon Valley rebels could not break certain laws.

Jake's under-powered subcompact rental car struggled up the continuously rising roadway. Traffic was light going through the mountain pass. He passed only a few cars on his way to the 3,800-foot summit at Loma Prieta Peak, epicenter of the magnitude 6.9 earthquake that interrupted Game 3 of the Major League Baseball 1989 World Series between cross-bay rivals, San Francisco Giants and Oakland Athletics. Jake felt the pull of gravity as he crested the apex, leading him toward the ocean.

The headlights of an impatient motorist behind him glared in his rearview mirrors. The lights grew larger, filling the interior of his cabin. Jake squinted at the road ahead, straining to follow the curves in the road and avoid being distracted by the tailgater.

Jake pressed the accelerator as he entered a straightaway. The car behind him crept closer. Jake gnashed his teeth. He hated tailgaters. If they were in a rush, they should have been in front of him. They drove in the right lane; the trailing car could have easily passed him on the left.

On a gradual left-hand bend, the tailgater jerked to the left and blazed past. The silhouette of the driver, a woman or a long-haired man, flashed by. Taillights faded into the distance. Jake sighed and concentrated on driving; his exit approached.

Another set of headlights glared in Jake's rearview mirrors. Another inconsiderate driver. High beams this time. The vehicle was big, not an eighteen-wheeler, possibly a large SUV. It appeared out of nowhere and quickly closed the gap. Jake pressed his accelerator harder. The SUV continued to close at an increasingly rapid rate.

Tires squealed as Jake's car teetered through a curve. The road swung to the left; Jake held the steering wheel tight. What's with the drivers out here?

The car behind him was within a few feet. Another right turn, tighter than the last. As Jake slowed to enter the curve, the SUV rammed his left rear bumper causing his car to slide off the pavement. Headlights flashed across tree trunks as his car spun out of control. His tires ground through the gravel along the shoulder, and the car plowed through the surrounding bushes, down an embankment, and crashed into a massive tree at the bottom of a ravine. His engine quit; headlights busted out.

Jake awoke to the smell of gasoline biting his nostrils. Seatbelt still fastened, he was suspended at a 45-degree, downward-facing angle, staring through his windshield, a spider's web of cracks. Shattered redwood branches stretched across his hood. Pinned between his collapsed seat back and the steering wheel, he tried to slide out. A stabbing pain pierced his rib cage. He aborted his escape attempt, gasped for breath, and passed out.

TWENTY-TWO

Tuesday, March 30

Jake awoke to a steady electronic beeping to his right. His lids fluttered as his eyes adjusted to the hazy white brightness. Voices in the distance sounded like they were at the far end of a long tunnel. Footsteps approached. Each step reverberated in his throbbing head.

"Good, you're awake," a woman in a white lab coat said as she entered the room. She shone a bright light in Jake's eyes. "I'm Doctor Mansfield. I'm your physician."

She peered at his pupils. "Good. No signs of brain damage," she said past the ringing in his ears.

He blinked to clear his blurred vision. Slowly, his focus returned, and he saw the dark-haired doctor checking the readouts of instruments next to his bed: blood pressure, pulse, blood oxygen levels. She nodded her approval.

"How do you feel?" the doctor asked in a mild Southern accent.

"I ache all over," Jake groaned. "Where am I?"

"Regional Medical Center," she replied, "in San Jose."

"What happened to me? How did I get here?"

"The paramedics brought you in last night. They found you off Highway 17. Do you remember being on that road?"

It hurt Jake's head to think. "I remember driving."

"What else do you remember?"

He closed his eyes, hoping it would help him recover his memories. He fought the nausea that was rumbling in his stomach. "Nothing."

"That's OK. It may take time for you to remember the details. Just relax. Nothing to worry about. Your vital signs are all normal. A broken rib and a concussion. The paramedics said your car ran through a lot of brush, slowing you down before hitting a tree. Your airbags deployed. They probably saved your life."

Jake touched his face with his hand and found bandages along his cheek and forehead.

"Airbag burns. The police found you thirty feet below the road down a ravine. A passing motorist witnessed the accident and called it in. You were lucky they got to you right away."

"Accident?"

"Yes, another car hit you from behind. That's how you ended up off the road," the doctor explained. "You don't remember it?"

Jake strained past the fuzziness in his head. "I remember bright lights."

"The police want to question you about the incident. I told them I'd let them know when that might be appropriate. I'll tell them you'll be ready to talk to them tomorrow."

A memory popped into his head. "Alexis!" She was in danger.

"Who's Alexis? Your wife? Girlfriend? Should we try to contact her?"

"No. I have to find her." Jake tried to sit up and grimaced. "Ow!" He held his left side.

"That would be your broken rib. Because of your concussion, I want you to stay another day for observation." She checked the readings on the instruments by his bed. "Rest. I'll check in on you in a few hours." She left him alone in the room.

Jake couldn't wait for the police. He had enough of the cops. If Martinez learned of his activities and his whereabouts, he'd be lectured again. Alexis was still with that monster. He had to find her.

Jake searched the room for his clothes, staggered to his feet, ears ringing, and furniture-surfed his way to the closet. He found his clothes neatly folded on a shelf, reached up with his right arm and dragged down his pants.

◆　◆　◆

Jake was once again on southbound Highway 17, re-tracing his path from the night before. Different this time, new rental car driving during daylight. The rental agency wasn't eager to issue him another car after totaling his last one and looking like he belonged in a hospital bed, not behind the wheel.

Jake drove past the point where he spun off the road; a section of torn shrubbery marked his exit. The pain in his head and ribs reminded him of the cost of the accident. It disturbed him he didn't remember being run off the road. He turned his attention back to his driving and exited the freeway a mile later.

Following instructions given by his GPS navigation system, Jake drove the winding route up the mountain through thick forests. About a mile from his destination, Jake lost his cell phone signal and Internet connection. His navigation app maintained contact with the GPS satellites and using the stored destination's coordinates led him through the tricky last few hundred yards.

The gravel road to Faulkner's cabin, carved into the slope of the mountain, was barely wide enough for two cars to pass. On Jake's left was a steep, rocky face, to his right, a drop-off to a canyon a hundred feet below. That fissure wasn't visible on the satellite photographs because of the thick canopy of the redwood forest dominating the hillside.

Jake passed only one house along the road — a rustic cabin perched on stilts on the mountain slope. A steep driveway led up to the house. Faulkner's cabin was a hundred yards ahead.

Jake cruised past the location given in the photo. He could barely make out a building on the right between the thick tree trunks and heavy brush lining the road. Tire tread marks on the ground between the bushes showed the way down an unpaved path to the structure. It was a perfect place to imprison someone — secluded. Jake continued cruising, searching for a place to hide his car.

Pine needles crunched under the tires as he pulled off the road fifty yards past Faulkner's hideout. Jake got out and hiked back down the road. When he reached the opening in the bushes, he hunched down and hugged the foliage as he snaked down the driveway.

The crude, single-story building was about forty feet across in the front and fifty feet deep. The front, constructed with wood siding painted dark brown, blended with the surrounding trees. Faulkner's car stood in the small clearing next to the cabin. There was a window in front with its curtains drawn. Jake crept around the right side. The wall resembled a medieval castle, made of stones, a hundred to two hundred pounds each. No windows or doors. He peeked around to the back wall. Same stone wall with no openings. He continued along the perimeter of the building toward the front. The left side was identical to the right. The only egress to the house was the front door. More secure than a jail — it was a safe.

Jake returned to the front porch and felt a vibration at his feet. He jumped around the side of the house, peeked around the corner, and watched the front door fly open. Faulkner bolted from the cabin, got into his car, and drove up to the road.

After the car was out of sight, Jake leapt around the corner and banged on the front door.

"Alexis! Are you in there?" He put his ear to the door. Nothing. He banged on the door again and jiggled the doorknob. It wouldn't budge. "Hold on, Alexis. I'll find something to break this lock."

Jake sprinted up the driveway, along the road, and back to his car. He opened the trunk and extracted a tire iron. He dashed back to the cabin with the makeshift lock pick in hand.

Jake jammed the pointed end of the lever between the door and the jamb and pushed it until the wooden frame cracked. He re-positioned his lever deeper into the gap and pushed again. The doorframe cracked and groaned until it snapped, and the door burst open.

Jake scanned the room. Amenities for one person. A sofa bed, a round table with one rickety chair, a small electric stove, and a plastic cooler. The back wall had a sturdy-looking metal door in the center. Jake checked the latch. Locked. He banged on it.

"Alexis! Are you in there?" he hammered on the door with the tire iron. He pressed his ear against the cold steel. Weak thumping, coming from the floor. "I'll get you out!" he yelled at the door.

Jake examined the door and its frame. Both made of metal. Faulkner's busybody neighbor said he was a handyman; he helped build a soundproof room at his condo complex. This cell was more of his handiwork. The metal door would not yield as easily as the front door. Jake ran his fingers along the edge of the door, searching for a place to wedge in his crowbar. The door had a narrow, even space all the way around. He stabbed the pointed end of his tire iron into the gap but couldn't get it in far enough. He examined the three heavy-duty hinges along the left side. They looked like they belonged on a bank vault, pins welded into place. It would take a blowtorch to remove them.

Jake laid down on the floor and peered through the narrow gap under the door. It was dark inside. The revolting smell of stale sweat and vomit leaked out. He yelled, "Alexis! Can you hear me?" A rustling sound.

Jake stood and stared at the door handle, designed to resist the heaviest assault. Heavy-duty, industrial-grade steel and fastened to the door with four large machine screws, heads filed down so that removing them was impossible without a wrench. If he had a chain, he could loop it around the handle, connect the other end to his car, and pull the handle off. Jake shook his head. Where would he find a chain in the wilderness?

The house he passed on his way up. The occupants might have a chain or tools to help free Alexis. Jake got off the floor.

Jake, on his hands and knees, heard something behind him. He turned in time to catch a fist to his jaw, sending spit and blood spraying across the room. Jake collapsed, dropped the tire iron, and fell to the floor.

Faulkner picked up the tire iron, raised it in both hands above his head, and swung it at Jake.

TWENTY-THREE

Tuesday, March 30

High above, branches swayed, slapping each other. Pine needles whistled, signaling the afternoon breeze from the ocean before the seasonal evening fog, signs of nature's tranquility, a contrast to the violence inside the cabin.

Jake's head spun, senses on overload; his jaw ached, vision blurred. Faulkner's punch came out of nowhere, landing squarely on Jake's cheek. Jake lay on his back, staring at the figure looming over him. Faulkner swung the tire iron like he was chopping wood.

Jake instinctively kicked up and caught Faulkner in the solar plexus. Faulkner grunted, and the iron clanged to the floor. Jake clambered to his feet and drove his shoulder into Faulkner's chest like a linebacker making a tackle. He sent Faulkner into the wall, forcing more air out of his lungs.

Faulkner landed a right hook into Jake's damaged ribs. Fiery pain jolted through Jake, doubling him over. Faulkner landed another blow to the back of Jake's head, crumpling him to his knees.

Faulkner turned to reach for the tire iron. Jake leapt at him, knocking him to the floor. The two men grappled on the floor, each trying to gain leverage.

Jake straddled Faulkner face-down on the floor. Jake clamped his forearm around his throat and squeezed. Army training kicked in. Faulkner twisted and kicked fruitlessly. Jake held a firm grasp, and in a minute, Faulkner stopped moving. Jake released his grip and checked his foe's pulse. He was unconscious but alive.

Jake checked Faulkner's pockets and found a set of keys, unlocked the metal door, and scanned the prison cell. Light flooded through the doorway, cutting across the floor to Alexis handcuffed to the wall on a thin mattress, dress soiled and torn. Jake rushed to her side, fumbled with the keys, unshackled her, and carried her out.

Jake handcuffed Faulkner's hands behind him and left him lying face-down on the floor. He turned his attention to Alexis. She was semi-conscious under the influence of the drugs Faulkner had given her.

Jake helped Alexis to a sitting position on the floor in the front room after tossing Faulkner into the prison cell. Alexis regained consciousness an hour later, but it took several minutes before she could speak.

"What happened?" Alexis groaned. She grabbed her sweat-laden hair. "My head feels like it's going to explode." She opened one eye. "Jake! Is that you?"

"Yes, Alexis. You're safe now." He sat next to her and wrapped his arm around her shoulder.

"Where are we?" she held her head with both hands as if trying to keep it from falling off. "The last thing I remember was going to that bar."

"We're in Faulkner's cabin in the Santa Cruz Mountains. He drugged you and brought you here."

Alexis looked around. "Where is he?"

Jake jerked his head toward the closed cell door. "I put him in there."

Alexis turned toward the metal door. "Did he have me in there?"

Jake nodded. "Let's get you out of here. You should see a doctor."

She examined Jake's face and said, "What happened to you?" She reached up to touch his scarred face.

Jake jerked back and winced from the pain in his ribs. "It's nothing. Can you stand?" Jake got off the floor and offered his hand.

"I think so." She grabbed his hand and hoisted herself to an unsteady standing position, leaning against him. "You're going to leave him in there?" She pointed to the cell.

"Yeah. He's not going anywhere. It's important that we get you to see a doc." Jake pulled on her arm toward the front door. She balked.

"Wait! What happened to Meghan? Did he kill her? Why? I need to find out the truth and I want to hear it from him." She pointed at the locked door.

Jake shook his head. "I don't think that's a good idea. I hate to say this, but we should leave this to the police now. Let them do their jobs and interrogate him." Bitterness grew in his mouth as he thought of his former rival, Martinez, taking over the investigation.

"No! He'll make some kind of deal with them and the truth won't come out. I need to find out what happened to my friend."

"I thought you were afraid of what the media might say, that they would twist the story around and blame her for what happened."

"He's a monster, and I hope he rots in prison, but before he does, I need to know what happened that night." She stared into Jake's face. "You feel the same way. You didn't go through all this trouble to hand it over to the police."

Jake bit his lip and sighed. She was right. He needed to know, too. He pulled out Faulkner's keys and walked to the cell door. He opened it and went inside. A moment later, he dragged a groggy and rubber-legged Faulkner into the front room and dropped him on the floor. Faulkner lay on his side, handcuffs still attached.

"What the hell?" Faulkner grumbled as he rolled on his back. He grimaced as the steel shackles bit into his wrists.

Jake hauled Faulkner by his shoulders and dragged him to a seated position against the wall. Jake and Alexis hovered over him.

"What happened the night Meghan disappeared?" Jake asked.

"I had nothing to do with her death," Faulkner replied.

"You lying son-of-a-bitch!" Alexis yelled. She kicked Faulkner in the ribs.

Faulkner fell over and screamed. "You whore!"

Alexis rushed at him and swung her foot at his head, missing by an inch.

Jake pulled Alexis aside, faced her, and held her shoulders. "Take it easy. Let him talk." He released his grip and turned back to Faulkner, who had righted himself. "Tell us. Did you kill Meghan?"

"I admit I picked her up at the park-and-ride near Crystal Springs, but I didn't kill her. It must have been that other guy!"

"What other guy?"

"He's lying. There was no one else. He's just trying to distract us," Alexis blurted.

Jake put his finger to his lips to instruct her to keep quiet. He turned back to Faulkner. "What guy? Who are you talking about?"

"The guy that rammed his SUV into us. He did it on purpose; I'm sure of it."

"Back up. Start from the beginning. What happened after you picked up Meghan?" Jake asked.

Faulkner took a deep breath and shook his head. "I'm not sure I should tell you. I should wait until I talk to my lawyer."

Alexis took a menacing step toward Faulkner. "You asshole!"

Jake put an arm out to hold her back. "I'm not a cop. I don't care about your Miranda rights. All I care about is finding Meghan's killer. If you don't talk to me now, I'll make sure the cops are all over your ass for every nasty thing you've done." Jake's eyes bored in on Faulkner.

Faulkner dropped his gaze. "OK. Here's what happened. After I picked her up, we drove south on 280."

Built in 1955, Interstate 290 was the freeway that connected San Francisco with San Jose; 57 miles meandering along the backbone of the San Francisco Peninsula in the scenic foothills. Unlike its baylands counterpart, Highway 101, I-280 avoided passing through the busy, commercial sections of the peninsula cities, instead passing mostly through protected wildlands. I-280 was wide and fast with sparse traffic.

"We were passing through Redwood City when this big SUV comes out of nowhere behind me and slams into my rear end. I lost control of my car and we skidded off the road."

A classic pursuit intervention technique or PIT maneuver; a technique used by law enforcement to force uncooperative suspect vehicles off the road. A tricky maneuver.

"What did the SUV look like?"

"Big. Black. I can't be certain. Possibly a Suburban or Escalade. I wasn't paying attention."

The incident reminded Jake of his accident on Highway 17. Faulkner's description matched the vehicle that hit Jake. Not a coincidence. "OK. Go on."

"I was shaken, but OK. I checked on Meghan. She had hit her head and was unconscious but alive. The other driver pulled over behind us and got out of his car. I was pissed and got out to confront him. As he approached, I knew I was in trouble. He was bigger than me, muscular. He punched me in the face. I'd never been hit so hard in my life. When I came to, Meghan and the SUV had disappeared."

Jake contained his anger with Faulkner. He should have called 911 immediately to help Meghan instead of picking a fight with the driver that caused the accident. Composing himself, Jake said, "What did this driver look like?"

Faulkner described the man who hit him. Jake nodded. It was time to get on another airplane.

TWENTY-FOUR

Jake gazed out his window, watching the snow-tipped Rocky Mountains skim past five miles below. His thoughts drifted to how things might have been different if she had listened to him. He did what he set out to do — he discovered what happened to Meghan. Her death was a tragedy, but learning who was responsible was surprising. The question that remained was: why?

Jake's plane made a gentle landing at the mile-high airport. He rented another car but didn't need the navigation system; he remembered the way from his previous trip. It was noon when he drove through the security gates and stopped in front of the mansion. A black Escalade stood in the driveway. Jake ran his hand along the front of the vehicle. The culprit was there.

A butler greeted Jake at the door and led him to the study. He waited as the servant advised his hosts of his arrival.

"What the hell are you doing back here!" Katherine demanded as she stormed into the room with Charles trailing.

"I know what happened to Meghan," Jake declared.

"You think you do, but you don't," Katherine shot back.

"Whatever happened to her is because of your actions, because of the stifling way you raised her. I blame you for her death."

"Me? I'm not responsible for her death. I gave her life. I gave her the best life anyone could ask for. I raised Meghan to be the perfect woman. She was perfect. She was beautiful, intelligent, obedient."

"Brilliant and beautiful, yes. But not obedient. Am I right?" Jake shot a glance at Charles, who seemed disinterested; he'd heard the arguments before.

"What the hell does that mean?" Katherine screeched.

"You said it yourself. She suffered from bipolar disorder. She was sweet and wonderful one second and rebellious the next. A lot of kids her age want to rebel, but she was different; wasn't she? Because of her psychological condition, you couldn't handle her; she got out of control."

Meghan exhibited risky, dangerous behavior that appeared in patients with untreated bipolar disorder. One notable example was an Olympic athlete that suffered from bipolar disorder manifested in hyper-sexuality.

The elite runner lived a double life: a professional racer by day, an escort by night. Doctors diagnosed her with a form of bipolar disorder that led to her unique personalities and unconventional lives. She also suffered from an overwhelming desire for sex, so her second, hidden life was that of a high-end Las Vegas escort. Apparently, the same obsessive drive that led to her success on the track fueled her desire for sex. Despite her notoriety as an Olympic athlete, she kept her secret for years.

"So what?"

"You needed help to contain the fallout from any negative attention she might have brought upon your precious reputation." Jake glanced at Charles. "That's when you hired Jameson."

"Jameson?" Katherine said innocently. "I hired him as my personal assistant. He has nothing to do with Meghan."

"That's a lie. You hired him to keep an eye on Meghan. You also hired him to clean up after her messes. You said, when Meghan left home for college, you couldn't control her; all you could do was to cover up any damage she caused. That's where Jameson came in; he was your fixer."

"Even if he did, so what? I couldn't have her ruin our reputation with her antics. We handled things our way, privately, quietly. The way we like it. There's nothing wrong with that."

Jake turned to Charles. "He parked his car out front. He's here. Call him."

Charles picked up the phone and called Jameson. A minute later, the PR man entered the study.

"Have you had any repair work done on your SUV?" Jake asked Jameson.

"Repair work? No." Katherine interrupted. "What repairs?"

"Jameson can explain," Jake said as he turned toward the hired hand.

Jameson stood silent, expressionless.

"As I walked in, I noticed the Escalade parked outside. It's yours, isn't it, Jameson? It's the one Charles lets you use for business."

Jameson nodded.

"I also noticed the fresh front-end work. Run into something?" Jake asked.

Jameson remained silent.

"Why don't you tell us what happened that night? The night you rammed Faulkner's car and abducted Meghan."

"What are you talking about? I wasn't there," Jameson protested.

"May I see you phone?" Jake asked with his palm outstretched.

Jameson turned toward Charles for support.

"Give it to him," Charles demanded.

Jameson reached into his pocket and handed his phone to Jake.

Jake scanned it. "I understand Charles bought this for you. With Charles's help, I got this list." He pulled a sheet of paper from his jacket.

Prior to flying to Denver, Jake contacted Charles to get information about a smartphone he purchased as a business expense.

"It's the GPS record of your phone at the time of Meghan's disappearance."

Jameson shifted his stance and crossed his arms. He raised his eyebrows.

Jake continued. "They match Meghan's locations that night. You were there when Faulkner's car got rear-ended. You caused that accident. That's why you had repair work done on the SUV." Jake tapped the page. "I bet if I looked deeper, I'll find that you were on Highway 17 at the time I got run off the road and sent to the hospital."

"I admit it. I hit his car. I did it to stop him. I didn't abduct her. I rescued her," Jameson spat. "Faulkner is a predator. A sex fiend. A pervert. He planned to enslave her. I couldn't let that happen."

Jameson excelled at his job. He not only kept track of Meghan's movements. He researched the people she met and dated, including a background check on Alexis, and warned Katherine about her sugar baby activities.

Jameson did a similar background search on Faulkner. He uncovered his sinister past and perverse relationships with women. Jameson convinced women who had dated Faulkner to confide in him and give him the sordid details of their affairs. Faulkner posed a threat to Meghan; he did what was necessary to protect her.

Katherine's face blanched; her mouth fell open. "What are you saying? You knew all along what had happened to her? Why didn't you tell us?" she staggered to the nearest chair and fell into it.

"Like two years ago. Remember?" Jameson asked Katherine. "I did my job."

Katherine turned away. Charles had a puzzled look on his face, his mouth agape.

"What happened two years ago?" Jake asked.

"Police arrested Meghan for solicitation. They instructed me to make the situation vanish. We ended up pressuring the police to drop the charges and paying off the guy to keep quiet," Jameson explained.

"How did you get the cops to drop the charges?"

Jameson looked at Katherine for guidance. She averted his gaze. He turned back to Jake and replied, "I dug up some dirt on the detective and blackmailed him." Jameson shrugged and glared at Katherine. "You told me to do whatever it took to keep her arrest out of the public eye. That's what I did."

"What happened after you hit Faulkner's car? What happened to Meghan?" Jake insisted.

"I had been following Meghan everywhere. I followed her on her trip to LA and arrived in San Jose on a flight just before hers. I followed her rideshare to the park-and-ride lot and saw her get into Faulkner's car. I had to take action. She was in danger and she didn't know it."

Jake nodded for him to proceed.

"They drove on the freeway heading away from the populated areas. I sensed Meghan was in deep trouble. I raced up behind them and I performed a PIT maneuver to get him off the road."

"You rammed their car? Like they taught you at the CHP?"

Jameson nodded and continued his story. "He got out and came at me; I punched him and knocked him out. The guy had a glass jaw. One punch and he crumpled like a house of cards. I found Meghan unconscious in the front seat. Her airbag had deployed and must have knocked her out. I put her in my car and drove away."

"Did she wake up in your car?"

"Yes. She flew into an uncontrollable rage. She screamed that I had interfered with her date. She demanded that I stop and let her out. I tried to reason with her while I drove, but she kept screaming, so I pulled over. As soon as we stopped, she got out and ran. I chased her and grabbed her, but she fell and hit her head on a rock. I checked for a pulse, but she was gone. There was nothing I could do."

"You killed her?" Katherine blurted.

"It was an accident. I didn't mean to harm her. I was trying to protect her."

Jameson had been unprepared for Meghan's accidental death and panicked. He had decided the best thing to do was to hide her body. He drove to the remote park and buried her body where he hoped no one would find her.

"It was rotten luck those hikers found her body. In a few weeks, this would have blown over," Jameson lamented.

Katherine slipped silently from the room. One nightmare had ended, but another was on its way.

"What happened to her phone?" Jake asked.

"I destroyed it," Jameson replied. "I knew she did everything on her phone. It had too much inflammatory evidence on it."

Jameson had reported to Katherine that he lost track of Meghan. After news of her disappearance broke, he recommended they not make any public statements believing the more the press heard from them, the more they'd want to dig for a juicy story. Silence was the key to preserve their pristine image. Since there were no ransom demands and no other evidence of foul play, he convinced Martinez that Meghan was a runaway.

Jake called the Denver police to take Jameson into custody. He willingly surrendered, a defeated man.

"I'll get him the best lawyer we can find for his defense. It was an accident," Charles told Jake after the police had departed. "It will take Katherine time to get over all this, but she'll prevail."

"I'm sure she will," Jake replied.

EPILOGUE

Sunday, April 12

White linens covered the round dining tables; elaborate floral arrangements of Meghan's favorites: roses, lilies, and lilacs adorned their centers. Silverware and napkins awaited the mourners. Caterers hustled to lay out the gourmet dishes on the serving tables along the reception hall walls. Servers opened bottles from a boutique Napa Valley winery rivalling the pedigree of any import.

As with every event Katherine planned, the reception after her daughter's memorial service was flawless. Despite having just two weeks to prepare for the event, she used her usual diligence and attention to detail. She scurried from one station to the next, her black dress flowing behind her, issuing precise directions to the staff, ensuring everything met her lofty standards.

The pastor had delivered a poignant sermon at the funeral in the chapel next door, memorable and moving, a fitting tribute to the young woman. He reminded the parishioners that life was fleeting and to cherish loved ones. His speech caused the women in the pews to cry in anguish, tears streamed down their faces dripping onto their designer shoes; the men choked back sobs. The eulogies were equally moving. Speakers espoused Meghan's accomplishments; they described her as a loving human being, someone who left them too soon. They said goodbye to the perfect little girl, mourning the loss of a loved and cherished soul. Alexis's words generated the loudest moans.

"Meghan left us too soon. A wonderful friend, daughter, granddaughter, niece. A beautiful soul. She told me once; life is like a train ride; you get on, ride a while, and get off. Along the way, you enjoy your fellow travelers and the scenery. If you're lucky, you make friends that last a lifetime. That was Meghan. My friend for life."

Katherine had told her guests Meghan would have wanted an elaborate funeral service. In fact, friends, family, and society expected it to honor Meghan and her life. For Katherine, the most important thing was to maintain appearances. She had done that through Meghan's life, and she would continue after her death. Protect image and reputation; to do otherwise would be disastrous.

After the service, mourners packed the church's social hall. Katherine seemed to relish people surrounding her. She had planned and hosted countless parties and social gatherings: soirées with members of the women's club, speaker engagements at the country club, and formal dinners at the Denver-area five-star restaurants. Her family's social status coupled with her husband's financial bearing made her the hub of activity among the elite. Her position afforded her great prestige, but with it came great responsibility to uphold a measure of decorum for her and her family. Socialites, perhaps driven by jealousy or pride, had little tolerance for cracks in their armor. Gossips seemed to lurk in every corner, waiting for some miscue to bring down the haughty.

Jake passed women chatting in hushed tones at the outer edges of the throng.

"She was always getting into trouble, even as a child," a woman with dyed brown hair said to the matron standing next to her. "Katherine always covered it up."

"I heard Katherine had to bail her out of jail in Nevada once," the matron replied. "I bet she got involved in something that got her killed." She turned and spotted Katherine standing too close. She nudged her friend, dipped her head, and slunk away.

Katherine bristled as she brushed past the gabby women. Gossips. Jealous gossips couldn't leave the dead alone. Despite her best efforts, the rumors leaked out; it grated on her.

"Did you hear they caught the other man?" A tall, thin woman sipped her chardonnay with her two friends.

A woman in a green dress shook her head. "It's terrible. She associated with all the wrong men. She should have stayed with Doctor Reinhardt. That's a fine match."

The tall woman nodded.

"What 'other man'?" the third gossip asked.

"His name was Faulkner. They charged him with kidnapping, rape, and false imprisonment of Meghan's roommate. The police are charging him with crimes against other women he abused over the years. Those other victims came forward after the news broke about his part in Meghan's death." The woman in green shuddered.

"What's his connection with Meghan?" The third gossip leaned in.

"He picked her up after her rideshare to the reservoir. He might have been trying to kidnap her." The tall woman slurped the last drops from her glass.

"Did you hear about the man that killed her?" the woman in green asked. "He worked for Katherine. How can she live with herself knowing she hired her daughter's killer?"

Katherine approached Jake. "Maybe you were right." Resignation in her voice. She shook her head. "I tried to raise her the best way I knew how. I guess that wasn't good enough."

I told you so echoed in Jake's head. Instead, he said, "She was beautiful and brilliant, but she was human. As a human, she had flaws. Flaws that probably cost her life."

"I tried to control her. I tried to contain the damage she caused. It wasn't enough."

Jake bit his tongue again. What Meghan needed was therapy, not someone to follow her and pick up the pieces when she did something embarrassing. She had a risky lifestyle; the odds caught up to her.

Kenzie, wearing a dark blue dress, glided across the glossy hardwood floor and joined them. The teenager said, "I'm so sorry, Aunt Katherine. I didn't know Meghan well, but I'll miss her; she was family and my only cousin."

"Thank you, dear." Katherine turned to Jake. "You've done a splendid job raising Kenzie. I can tell. She stands tall, confident. She's smart and brave. She will go far."

Jake nodded and wrapped his arm around his precious daughter. "She wants to go to Stanford, just like Meghan. She looked up to her." He squeezed Kenzie. "You're right. She will go far. I hope I haven't held her back."

Kenzie smiled. "I have lots of other schools on my list. Stanford's expensive and far from home. Maryland is a great school; close to home; and my friends are including it on their lists."

Jake opened his mouth to argue, but his phone buzzed. A text message from Tim McGuire. "It's the reporter from Stockton. I've got an interview with him tomorrow."

"That's great, Dad. It should be good advertising." Kenzie grinned and nudged her father.

Before Jake could counter her comment, a stranger interrupted.

A well-dressed man approached them. "My condolences, Katherine."

"Thank you, Geoffrey. Have you met my brother, Jake, and his daughter, Kenzie?"

"Hello, Mr. Granger. I'm Geoffrey Kendall." He shook Jake's hand and nodded to Kenzie. "I am so sorry for your loss. I've known Charles and Katherine for many years. I watched Meghan grow up."

Jake released his grip. "Thank you very much. We will all miss her."

"I realize this may not be the most appropriate time or place, but I was hoping to talk to you about a problem I have."

Jake scrunched his face. "Problem?"

"This is where I take my leave," Katherine said. She smiled at her old friend. "Thank you for coming today, Geoffrey." She strode toward a gaggle of women dressed as if they were attending an Easter event.

"I'll see you later, Dad." Kenzie slid toward a group of girls assembled near the buffet.

"I'll see you later." Jake turned to Geoffrey and asked, "What can I do for you?"

"Jake, I'm responsible for running the IT operations for my company. We have several locations including Denver, Washington, and New York." He looked around and continued in a lower tone. "Hackers attacked us; they got to our customer private information. We desperately need someone to identify and fix the weaknesses in our computers and networks."

Jake's eyes widened. "I would definitely be interested in talking with you."

"Excellent! Here is my card. Please contact my office to set up a meeting to discuss the details." They exchanged business cards. "Thank you very much."

Jake shook Kendall's hand and glanced at Katherine. She gave him a Mona Lisa smile. Bumping into Geoffrey was not a chance encounter; Katherine had set up the meeting. He nodded back, thanking her for the introduction. Kenzie could put Stanford back on her list.

ACKNOWLEDGMENTS

This story was written in memory of Mackenzie Lueck. The circumstances of her disappearance and tragic death in 2019 led to the creation of this fiction.

Thank you to my beta readers: Doreen, Heidi, Rebecca, Tahmina, and Zoe. They encouraged me and reminded me of the key rules to writing good fiction.

I thank my friends and family for encouraging my writing. I especially thank my wife, Naomi, for always supporting me.

ABOUT THE AUTHOR

Wesley Hisao Higaki published his first book in 2010, a technical guide for product developers based on his experiences at Symantec Corporation. He shared his lessons learned, translating security jargon into language product developers could easily understand.

He began writing fiction as a fresh challenge. He wanted to write stories he liked to read — suspenseful with accurate depictions of modern technology. He uses his formal education — bachelor's degree in math from the University of California, Davis and masters in computer science from Santa Clara University — and his 30 years of work experience in Silicon Valley, to write interesting fiction using technology in supporting roles presented in understandable ways to a broad audience while satisfying technophiles.

He can be reached through his Facebook author's page at www.facebook.com/whigakiauthor or on his blog at www.wesleyhisaohigaki.wordpress.com.

Find his other titles on his Amazon Author's page at www.amazon.com/author/wesleyhisaohigaki.